WHEN THE
WORLD
WAS
OURS

LIZ KESSLER

ALADDIN
NEW YORK   LONDON   TORONTO   SYDNEY   NEW DELHI

ALADDIN
An imprint of Simon & Schuster Children's Publishing Division
1230 Avenue of the Americas, New York, New York 10020
First Aladdin hardcover edition May 2021
Text copyright © 2021 by Liz Kessler
Originally published in Great Britain in 2021 by Simon & Schuster UK Ltd.
Jacket illustration copyright © 2021 by Matt Saunders
All rights reserved, including the right of reproduction in whole or in part in any form.
ALADDIN and related logo are registered trademarks of Simon & Schuster, Inc.
For information about special discounts for bulk purchases, please contact Simon & Schuster
Special Sales at 1-866-506-1949 or business@simonandschuster.com.
The Simon & Schuster Speakers Bureau can bring authors to your live event. For more information
or to book an event contact the Simon & Schuster Speakers Bureau at 1-866-248-3049 or visit our
website at www.simonspeakers.com.
Designed by Heather Palisi
The text of this book was set in Goudy Oldstyle.
Manufactured in the United States of America 0421 FFG
2 4 6 8 10 9 7 5 3 1
Library of Congress Control Number 2020949941
ISBN 9781534499652 (hc)
ISBN 9781534499676 (ebook)

For my dad, Harry Kessler, my guiding light and inspiration in so many ways.

Also for Mr. and Mrs. Jones (the original "Mr. & Mrs. Stewart"), whose extraordinary act of generosity saved my family's lives and allowed me to be here today to tell this story.

And for my grandparents, Mama and Papa, because this was your story too.

A NOTE FROM THE AUTHOR

My father was eight years old when he left Nazi-occupied Czechoslovakia with his parents, Frank and Annie, in 1939. As a Jewish family their options were severely limited—almost nonexistent—at that point. The thing that led to their escape was a letter from a British couple they had met five years earlier. The couple only met them because my father had nearly scuffed the woman's dress, and my grandfather had warned him to be careful. This moment led to a conversation, a day spent together, and a thank-you letter that would later save their lives.

This story has been an influence and a guiding light throughout my life, and for many years I have wanted to write a book inspired by it. Leo's narrative is the one that was inspired by my father's story, but my family's history has influenced other aspects of this novel too. My great-aunt Elsa was murdered at Auschwitz, and my great-grandmother Omama spent four years at Theresienstadt.

Elsa's story comes from the many times I've asked myself what might have happened to my family if they hadn't had that extraordinary stroke of luck. And Max's story is my attempt to explore how so many ordinary people could have become part of such a brutal, evil, and horrific regime.

This book is not only a way for me to honor my past, my ancestors, and my heritage. It is also about using my voice to contribute to the conversations about social justice taking place today, and hopefully help young readers make informed decisions about the part they want to play in the world of tomorrow.

CONTENT WARNING

This story contains mature themes and depictions of violence and cruelty related to the Holocaust, and we advise readers to be aware of difficult content that may cause distress. A list of resources with more information on the Holocaust and this period in history can be found at the end of this book.

WHEN THE WORLD WAS OURS

1936

Leo

I could see the whole world! Or at least the whole of Vienna, and that *was* my world.

My two best friends, Max and Elsa, stood beside me, their faces pressed to the glass next to mine.

"Look at the tiny people!" Max exclaimed, pointing down below us as we rose higher and higher into the sky.

"The buildings look like a toy town!" Elsa said.

I couldn't even speak. I was too afraid that if I opened my mouth, some of the joy inside me might slip out, and I didn't want to lose a single bit of it.

It was my ninth birthday and the best day of my life, bar none.

When my parents had asked me last week what I wanted to do for my birthday, there was no contest. I wanted to ride on Vienna's Ferris wheel: the Riesenrad. We had lived in Vienna almost my whole life, but I'd never been on it. Whenever I asked, Mama would always say I was too young and that I'd be afraid to be so high up. But I wasn't scared at all. I think Mama was afraid herself, really, which is why she decided she wouldn't come with us.

"Your papa will take you to the fairground," she told me. "I'll stay home and prepare a wonderful birthday meal for you. What cake would you like?"

"Sachertorte!" I replied without hesitating. Mama made the best Sachertorte in Vienna. She had a secret recipe, passed down from Omama, my grandma.

I crossed the days off on the calendar in the kitchen. The week crawled by slower than the snails at the bottom of our garden.

But now at last my birthday was here, and the Riesenrad ride was even better than I'd imagined it would be. It was a cold October day, but bright and sunny and we could see for miles and miles.

The carriage rose higher and higher. We would soon be in the clouds!

Max leaned his forehead against the window. "I feel like the king of Vienna," he said. The glass fogged up as he spoke.

I knew what he meant. Climbing high above the city made me feel invincible. Vienna was ours to share. A whole city spread out just for Elsa, Max, and me. All the other people in the carriage had faded into the background. Even Papa. He was sitting reading a newspaper and frowning. He was missing the best thing in the world!

We didn't care. The fact that the adults were missing out only kept more of it for us. Our city, this carriage, our friendship—that was all we needed.

It was always like that with us three. We'd been best friends since the first day of *Volksschule*—big school—two years ago. We had been seated in a row of three, Elsa in between Max and me like she was now. I can still picture us: me with my tie done up so tightly I could hardly breathe; Elsa with her plaited hair and pink ribbons and her pencil case with shiny beads; Max in his trousers that were just a little too short and his shirt that was a little too big.

We looked at each other that first morning and smiled, and it was as if we knew it straightaway: we were a team. When the boys pulled on my tie, when they laughed at Max's ankles sticking out of the bottom of his trousers, when the girls made fun of Elsa's fancy ribbons—none of it mattered because we had each other.

"If you're the king, I'll be queen," Elsa said now.

"What about me?" I asked. "It is my birthday, after all."

"We can have two kings!" Elsa replied. That was so like her. Always wanting to be fair to everyone.

"If you're the queen, that means you have to marry one of us," Max said. "So who will you choose?" He gave Elsa a look as he spoke. A look that I'd seen between them sometimes recently. I always pretended I hadn't noticed. It felt like a secret they shared. A promise that excluded me. I told myself I was imagining it. They would never exclude me. Nothing would ever come between the three of us.

Elsa giggled. "I could never choose!" she said. "I'll marry you both, of course."

That was good enough for me.

Max folded his arms and narrowed his eyes as he pretended to think. "Okay, that's an excellent plan," he said, nodding his agreement.

"Hey, kids." Papa folded up his paper and cupped his ear. "Can you hear that?"

We strained to listen. Other than the soft chatter of the other people in the carriage, I couldn't hear anything. "What are we listening to?" I asked.

Papa laughed. "Nothing! That's just it. It's the sound you hear when the carriage stops."

He was right. The big wheel was still and now we were on top of the whole world. For a moment, I wondered if we might stay there forever. I hoped so.

Then I remembered Mama's Sachertorte waiting for us at home and decided that forever might be a little too long.

Papa had stood up and was getting his camera out of his jacket pocket. He rarely went anywhere without a camera. Papa was Vienna's finest family photographer. That's what it said on his shop window anyway.

"Come on, let's take your picture while you're on top of the world, eh?" he said.

The three of us squashed together in front of the window.

Papa lowered his camera and frowned. "Not there," he said. "The sun is right behind you. You'll be nothing but shadows. Come here." He waved a hand toward the door at the far end of the carriage. "Stand against this so the bright sky is in front of you."

We shuffled to the end of the carriage and squeezed in toward each other.

Papa looked at us through the camera's lens. "Perfect," he said. "We have to get the picture *just* right. And you know why that is?" he asked.

"Because a picture paints a thousand words," I replied, pretending to yawn. Papa said the same thing every time he took a photo.

He laughed. "That's right. And believe me, this *will* be a picture to paint a thousand words—all of them happy ones as well!" he said. "Now remember, whatever you do, *don't* smile!"

Max frowned. "I thought people *always* smiled in photos."

"Not in *my* photos," Papa replied in a mock serious tone. "I don't allow it."

Elsa let out a giggle.

"Ah ah! No laughing either!" Papa warned.

Elsa giggled again. I could feel my own face twitching into a smile.

"I said NO smiling!" Papa said again. By this time, everyone in the carriage was laughing, not just the three of us.

Click, click, click went the shutter.

"Beautiful, fantastic, wonderful!" Papa called as he photographed us, talking to us just like I'd heard him talk to his clients. When he'd finished, he lowered the camera. "I'll choose the best photo and give each of you a copy, so you'll always have a memory of this day. How does that sound?"

"It sounds wonderful, Papa," I said. "Thank you!"

"Good. Now then," he said as he put his camera back into his jacket pocket, "I think I saw at least one of you smiling. And you know how I punish smilers?"

Elsa shook her head. Max bit his lip. I knew what was coming and had already started to move away.

"I punish them with tickles!" Papa announced.

He reached out toward us, and all three of us squealed as we tried to run from his clutches. At that exact moment, the Ferris wheel started moving again and the carriage jolted. I fell forward and tripped over a lady's outstretched foot. The man next to her grabbed hold of me just before I landed in his lap.

Papa was beside me in a second. "I'm so sorry," he said to the couple. Then he looked down at me. "Leo, apologize to the lady."

I cleared my throat and tucked my shirt back under my suspenders. It had become ruffled as I'd fallen. "I'm really sorry," I said, looking the lady in the eye. For a moment, she stared at me so hard I thought she was going to tell me off. Then she turned to the man and said something in a different language. German was the only language I knew, so I couldn't understand what she was saying.

He replied in that other language, and then she nodded and turned back to me.

Waving both hands in front of her, she said, in broken German this time, "It okay. Nothing. No mind." I didn't understand exactly what she meant, but her words were accompanied with such a big smile that I knew I was off the hook. "We are English," she added. "Not speak good German."

"You speak very well," Papa replied. Then he turned back to me. "And what do you say to the gentleman who stopped you from falling?" he prompted.

"I'm sorry," I said to the man. "And thank you."

The man gave me a broad smile and waved a hand as if to dismiss my apology. Then the woman spoke to Papa. "Your son?" she said.

"Yes, he's my son," Papa replied. "He's nine today." Gesticulating to indicate the ride, he said, "Birthday treat!"

"Ah!" The woman turned back to me.

"Happy birthday," the man said with another broad smile.

"He is beautiful boy," the lady said. She pointed at my hair.

Beautiful? Who called boys beautiful? Maybe it was because of my blond curls.

"Can I go now?" I asked Papa.

"Yes, but be more careful, okay? No more bumping into people."

I didn't say that I'd only bumped into them because he'd been chasing us with tickle hands. I could see Max and Elsa huddled up together, and I wanted to get back to them. I didn't want to miss out on even one minute of this day.

"Sit with us. Please," the woman was saying to Papa as I moved away.

"If you're sure," Papa replied. He reached out to shake her hand. "I am Frank Grunberg," he said.

"Aileen Stewart," said the lady. Then she pointed at the man. "Eric Stewart, my husband."

"Please to meet you," the man said in broken German like his wife's as he shook Papa's hand.

Papa sat down beside them, and before I'd even gotten back to Max and Elsa, he was talking animatedly with the couple.

That's what he was like. He could talk to anyone, even people who didn't speak the same language! Everyone loved my father. Everyone smiled when he was around, and wanted to be his friend. Sometimes I wished I was like that, but mostly I was fine how I was. I had my two best friends. I didn't need any more. The three of us were enough for each other.

The ride had come to an end and people were piling out of the carriage. Papa was still deep in conversation with the English couple. None of them had noticed we were back on the ground.

"Mister. You going around again?" the man at the door said.

Papa looked up. His eyes twinkled like they always did when

10

he had an idea. "You know what?" he said. "Yes! Let's go around again. What do you think, kids?"

We cheered, loud enough to make Papa cover his ears as he laughed. Then he turned to the couple next to him. "Come around again," he said, drawing a big circle in the air with his hand. "My treat. To apologize."

The man shook his head. "No. No," he said. "Not need to do that."

"Not need to," Papa replied. "*Want* to!"

Laughing, the couple shrugged and agreed to go around again. Papa stood up and went over to the door. He handed over a bunch of notes, and the ticket man shrugged. Then he let a few more people in, closed the door behind them, and off we went, back to the sky.

Elsa, Max, and I ran back to the window so we wouldn't miss a second as we soared up above the city once again.

That's what Papa could do. Take the best day ever and double it.

Elsa

When I grow up, I am going to be Mrs. Stewart.

I won't be called "Mrs. Stewart," of course, because I won't be married to Mr. Stewart. I will be married to either Max or Leo, so I suppose I will be called either Mrs. Fischer or Mrs. Grunberg. But I will be glamorous like Mrs. Stewart, and I will laugh like her and smile like her and pat my husband's arm like she does.

Max and Leo are jabbing their fingers against the window. "Look, that's my street!" Max exclaims. "I'm sure it is. There's the pink house on the corner!"

"That's city hall! There's the park!" Leo replies.

But we've been round once already and it looks just the same this time, so I would rather watch Mrs. Stewart.

She's probably about the same age as Mutti, but they are a world apart. Mrs. Stewart is wearing a red dress that looks as if she put it on especially to match the red of the carriage we're riding in. I bet she has a different dress for every occasion. She's wearing a red beret, and over her shoulders is a brown shawl that is so furry I thought at first that it was alive.

Until this moment, I'd thought Leo's mother was the most glamorous lady in Vienna. She always has perfectly coiffed hair, not a single curl out of place. She must have a different shade of lipstick for each day of the week, and always paints it onto her smiling mouth with perfection. Her eyes dazzle with brightly colored eye shadow. Whenever we're at Leo's house, I'm torn between playing with the boys and sitting and looking at her.

Sometimes I pretend she's a movie star and that she notices me and tells me I'm destined to be a star too. Other times, she is a fashion icon impressed by my designs and we walk the boards together in our fine outfits and colorful hats.

In reality, usually Mrs. Grunberg just winks at me and laughs as she squeezes my cheeks, and I run back to the boys.

But Mrs. Stewart—she has something on top of all that. Is it that her clothes are even brighter? Or that she laughs even harder? Whatever it is, I can't stop watching her.

She is so different from my own dear Mutti. My mother only ever seems to wear gray nowadays. At least, if I picture her, that's what I see. Gray or black. She doesn't wear any color. She used to. Not like Mrs. Stewart or Mrs. Grunberg, even. More like the other women in this carriage, with their suits and hats and nice shoes. But now: only gray and black. And her eyes are dark to match her clothes.

Yesterday I overheard her and Vati—my father—talking in low voices in the kitchen. I was on the landing, crouched down behind the banister so I could hear them without being noticed.

"You look like you're in mourning," Vati said.

"Maybe I am," Mutti replied.

"Who for?" Vati asked.

There was a long pause after that. I strained to listen, and eventually I heard Mutti say, "For all of us."

I didn't know what she meant by that, but they didn't speak again for a bit. I went downstairs a few moments later. Mutti and Vati were sitting at the table. Vati had his hand over Mutti's. She looked across when she saw me come in; then she quickly got up and went to the sink. As she passed me, I could see that her eyes were wet. I followed her to the sink and put my arms around her waist. "Are you all right, Mutti?"

She gripped my hands and squeezed them so hard it hurt a bit. Then she turned round, wiped her eyes, and ruffled my hair. "I'm fine, darling," she said. "Now go and tell your brother it's dinnertime."

That meant: don't ask any more questions. It's like that all the time at home lately. Overheard snippets of conversations between my parents that I don't understand and that clearly neither of them wants to talk about to me or Otto. Otto is my brother. He's two years older than me, and after Leo and Max he's my favorite boy in the world.

Otto doesn't ask as many questions as I do. He's more interested in finding broken things and fixing them. He's never happier than when he gets to spend hours with two planks of wood, a hammer, and a box of nails. He takes after Vati. Vati's a building contractor, so fixing things is his job. In Otto's case, the things he fixes often end up even more broken once he's done with them!

I sometimes wonder if Otto likes fixing things so much because he never fully fixed his leg after he fell out of a tree when he was five years old. He broke it in three places and had plaster all the way down his leg for the whole summer. The bones mended, but he's always had a slight limp since then. He hides it pretty well, and only mentions it very occasionally. "I wish I could make my leg as perfect as this shelf!" he'll say, but he's not complaining when he says things like that. He's usually hinting for us to admire his work!

He hasn't said anything about the way things have changed at home, but I know he's noticed it too. I can feel it from him, even in his silence.

It wasn't always like this. I can't even remember *when* it changed, but it seems like a really long time since I last saw Mutti smile.

Not like Mrs. Stewart.

Mrs. Stewart smiles *all* the time. She smiles while Mr. Grunberg talks; she smiles at her husband; she smiles even while she's talking. I make a note to practice that in front of a mirror. Smiling and talking at the same time: I bet it's quite a skill.

One of the men says something funny, and Mrs. Stewart throws back her head and laughs so heartily it's like an infection that spreads through the carriage, making everyone around her smile and laugh too.

I have a sudden memory.

Mutti and Vati in the kitchen, dishes on the table still to be washed, Vati's arm around Mutti's waist. There is music from somewhere. A waltz, I think. My grandparents were still alive then. I remember Grandpa tapping his foot to the rhythm, Grandma smiling and nodding with the music. Vati lifting an arm and Mutti twirling around beneath it before coming back into his arms.

The music ending, Vati taking a bow and Mutti laughing before returning to the table to pile the dishes up.

The memory hurts in my tummy. It feels so distant now.

I'll ask Mutti tonight if she remembers. See if it makes her smile when I tell her. I'll ask if she and Vati will dance in the kitchen again. I'll tell her how pretty she used to look when she smiled. That might make her do it more often.

I haven't realized that I'm still staring, and Mrs. Stewart catches me looking at her. Her mouth widens in another smile, this one especially for me. I feel my face burning as I quickly turn back to the boys.

"Let's remember this day forever and ever," I say, holding out a little finger to each of them. "Let's promise never to forget the day we were kings and queen of all of Vienna."

The boys grin at me and take a finger each. "Promise," they say in unison.

Our fingers stay linked for the rest of the ride.

Max

Max had never had a day like this. A day filled with so much laughter and happiness he was sure that if they opened the doors at the top of the ride, he would float even higher than the wheel itself.

It wasn't just the laughter that filled him up inside. He could have been anywhere in the world and it would have been a perfect day as long as he shared it with his two best friends.

Sometimes he tried to remember his life without Leo and Elsa. Even though they had only met when they'd started *Volksschule* a couple of years earlier, it felt as though they had been best friends forever.

When he did think about life before his best friends, the memories weren't happy ones. He remembered being alone in his bedroom with his hands over his ears to shut out the sound of his parents arguing downstairs: his father ranting and shouting and his mother trying to calm him down. It was always about the same thing: money. The fact that they never had enough since his father had lost his job when the company he worked for went out of business.

Max's mother always said that they had just enough to live on. But it was never good enough for his father. He was too proud to settle for "just enough." And so he ranted and raged and blamed everyone except himself, and Max shut himself in his room and covered his ears and waited for the arguments to end.

Kindergarten was no escape. He wished his mother would buy his school uniform from the same shop as everyone else rather than sew it from cloth that didn't quite match and was always slightly the wrong shape. The other kids laughed at him, and Max learned to manage without needing praise or friends or smiles. By the time his father got a new job and they could afford a proper school uniform, it was too late. The other children saw him as an outcast, a joke. That had changed when he met Elsa and Leo. They didn't judge him, and they were the only friends he needed.

But he wished his father would smile like this English couple, or talk to him and tease him like Leo's father did.

Max wasn't sure he could remember the last time his father had even looked at him. Nowadays he always seemed to be at work. Even in the evenings he was at meetings or with people from his office. He never talked about his job. But then, he never talked to Max much at all, other than to criticize him for one thing or another.

So days like these, times with his best friends, they were the most precious things that Max had—or could ever want.

"Come on, Triple Trouble," Leo's father said as they filed out of the carriage together, with a wink to show he didn't really think they were trouble. Max smiled. He liked it when Mr. Grunberg made jokey comments. Max's father *never* made jokes. Since he'd started his new job, he had become obsessed with efficiency and discipline. He once told Max that jokes were a waste of important time, only indulged in by people with nothing better to do.

Mr. Grunberg believed the opposite, Max could tell. He was like an always-full happiness machine that gave out laughter tokens to anyone who passed by.

"Ah!" The lady Mr. Grunberg had been talking to clasped a hand over her mouth. She said something in English and pointed at her watch.

"Everything all right?" Leo's father asked.

"We miss meeting!"

"What meeting was that?" Mr. Grunberg asked.

"We plan to catch tram after big wheel. Go to talk," she replied. "Too much fun, so we forget about it!"

"What's the talk?" Mr. Grunberg asked.

"Um. It's difficult in German. About tooth," the man said, pointing at his mouth.

"Mr. Stewart is dentist," the lady added. "Talk is about—what is the word?" She pointed under her teeth.

"Gums?" Mr. Grunberg suggested.

"Yes. Bad gum."

"Gum disease?"

"That's right," the man said.

"Oh. Well, that *does* sound exciting!" Leo's father said before turning round to the children and pulling a face that made them laugh. Max laughed the hardest. He loved the way Mr. Grunberg made them all feel included, as though they were all part of the same gang. Max couldn't get enough of that feeling.

"Maybe we will be in time for end of talk . . . ," the woman said, raising an eyebrow at her husband.

"Or maybe we miss the talk and stay at the fairground," the man replied.

His wife clapped her hands. "Wonderful idea!" she said. "Yes!"

"Well, now that's settled, you must stay with us a bit longer," Mr. Grunberg said. "And maybe you could come home with us after we've all had enough of the fair."

The couple stared at him. "Home with you?"

Mr. Grunberg leaned in as though he were sharing a state secret. "You have not experienced the real Vienna until you have tasted my wife's Sachertorte," he said. "Leo, you don't mind sharing your birthday cake with two more guests, do you?"

"Not at all, Papa," Leo replied.

"How about you kids—any objections?" Mr. Grunberg addressed Elsa and Max.

Max wanted to ask how much cake there was going to be. He'd had tea at Leo's house a few times, but he'd never had Mrs. Grunberg's Sachertorte. Leo had told them how wonderful it was, though, and Max was nervous that there might not be enough to go around now that there were two more to feed—and he was terrified he might be the one to lose out.

But then Elsa spoke for both of them. "We don't mind at all, Mr. Grunberg," she said, and Leo's father was ruffling Max's hair in a way his own father never did, and saying, "Good kids. Maybe we can go for a ride on the Steamer as a treat before we go home," and the warm feeling Max felt suddenly meant it didn't even matter if there was a bit less cake to go around.

The only thing that really mattered was that, later, as he and his friends jumped on the boat and sat together watching the city go by, the bonds of their friendship felt as deep and as wide as the Danube itself.

Leo

It was Saturday morning a few weeks later, and I was awake and dressed before my parents. That never happened! Except it did today because I couldn't sleep. I was too excited. Max's father was taking Max, Elsa, and me swimming at the Amalienbad.

In his car!

No one we knew had a car! I couldn't decide which I was more excited about: riding through Vienna in a car, spending the morning with my best friends, or the diving boards at the Amalienbad. It was a close call.

I had my bag ready, with swimming trunks rolled inside my towel, and I sat waiting near the window so I could look out for them. Mama was in the kitchen, baking. Papa was upstairs in his studio.

Finally, on the dot of ten o'clock, the car came around the corner and onto our street.

I bounced out of my chair so fast it made Mama jump. "They're here!" I yelled as I grabbed my bag.

"Wait. Let me give you these," she said as I ran into the kitchen to say goodbye. She handed me something in a small paper bag. It was warm.

"What's this?" I asked.

"*Kipferl*. Cookies for after swimming."

I threw my arms around her waist. "Thanks, Mama."

She kissed the top of my head. "Have fun with your friends," she said.

Papa came to the door with me. Max had thrown the back door of the car open and was grinning like an idiot. Elsa was on the other side and waved me over. "Come on!" Max called. "Let's go!"

Papa walked me to the car, then approached the front window where Mr. Fischer was sitting. Mr. Fischer didn't even look at him. He mustn't have noticed Papa.

"Shuffle up, then," I said to Max.

Papa was tapping on the front window. Eventually Mr. Fischer opened it a crack.

"How are you?" Papa asked him. "We haven't seen you for a while."

Papa had only met Mr. Fischer a few times. The first time was when we had just started at *Volksschule*. Mama and Papa wanted to meet my friends and their parents, and it had been a nice evening. Papa and Mr. Fischer had drunk wine and sat talking together.

Mrs. Fischer complimented Mama on her cooking. We all laughed a lot. It was a happy sort of evening. Mama said she was sure that they were going to become firm friends.

The next time they met was in the park when we bumped into them a few months later. Papa was all big smiles as usual, but Mr. Fischer had seemed a bit stiff. Papa dropped a jokey hint about it being their turn to host us for dinner, and the Fischers nodded and said they would invite us soon.

But they never did, and the firm friendship never happened. Mama worried about it, questioning why, and wondering if we had offended them somehow, but Papa said it was just one of those things and that everyone was busy nowadays.

But now, the way Mr. Fischer was sitting stiffly in his seat, barely looking at Papa, I found myself wondering if Mama was right.

"I am well," Mr. Fischer replied curtly. "We need to go now." Then he turned his head back to me. "Get in, boy, and shut the door."

I raised my eyebrows at Max and Elsa as I squeezed in beside them. Elsa gave a big shrug. Max just rolled his eyes.

And then Mr. Fischer started the engine, and as the car growled into life and trundled down the road, the three of us were back in our own world, talking nonstop, teasing each other, sharing cookies and secrets, and I forgot everything else.

Almost everything.

I couldn't help noticing Papa's face as he waved us off. He smiled as he always did—but it looked different from his usual smile. His eyes didn't twinkle. His eyes looked sad. I wondered if it was because of how Mr. Fischer had spoken to us, and I couldn't help asking myself the question it looked as if Papa was asking himself too.

What had we done wrong?

Elsa

I think the Amalienbad is the most beautiful building I have ever seen. I don't know which I like more: the perfect symmetry of the changing cubicles, layered in rows, one above the other; the deep, sparkling blue of the water; the light fanning through the windows in the domed ceiling—or the variety of swimming costumes all around me!

The boys are busy lining up for their turn on the diving board, and I'm sitting on the side of the pool, feet dangling in the water, watching a group of older girls near me. One of them has a costume that looks as if it's made from white silk. Another has one with the thinnest shoulder straps and large printed flowers all over it.

I feel frumpy in my plain, black costume.

"Elsa! Elsa!" Leo is calling to me. He's next on the diving board. "Watch me!"

Turning from the girls, I watch as he spreads his arms out and, without seeming to make any effort, arcs perfectly into the water. He swims underwater all the way to me and breaks the surface, wiping his hair off his face. "How did I do?" he asks, grinning as he treads water in front of me.

"Hmmm. Maybe seven out of ten!"

"Seven! Meanie!" Leo replies and splashes my legs. "Come on," he says, grabbing my feet. "Get in!"

"Hey! My turn!" Max calls.

I slide into the water, and we both cling to the side as we watch Max walk to the end of the board. He looks so small compared to the boys waiting behind him, and I see them looking at him and sniggering. My heart fills with pain for him—but he hasn't noticed the boys. He's too busy concentrating on his dive.

Max raises his hands in perfect straight lines above his head, slowly bends his knees, crouches forward and . . .

SPLASH!

He belly flops into the water. The boys behind him don't even hide their laughter now. Luckily, Max is still underwater, and by the time he reaches us, they've moved on to their own dives.

"Ten out of ten!" I say as he reaches us and grabs the side of the pool.

"You're just being kind," Max says.

27

"No. It was great." Leo agrees with me so quickly that I'm sure he must have seen the older boys laughing too. Then he pulls himself out of the water and grabs a ball from the benches on the side. "Here, let's play with this."

We swim to a quiet part of the pool and throw the ball between us, racing to be the one to catch it, laughing each time one of us misses it and takes a dunking, playing dolphin rides and bulldogs and every other game we manage to squeeze into our hour.

Too soon, someone blows a whistle and it's our turn to get out.

"Let's come again next week," Leo says as we make our way up to the changing cubicles.

"And the week after that," Max agrees.

"And every week after that forever," I add.

The boys each hold out a hand and I do the same, and we link fingers in a promise that we will always, always do everything together, no matter what.

Max

Max gave his hair one last rub and hung up his towel and swimming trunks in the airing cupboard before going to join his parents.

He and his friends had agreed to meet at the park after lunch, and he wanted to eat and get back out to play as quickly as possible.

He was heading downstairs when he heard raised voices from the kitchen.

Max froze on the bottom step. His father was clearly in the middle of a rant, and Max suddenly wasn't in quite such a hurry to join his parents.

"You should have seen his face when he saw me!" he heard his father say. "He thinks he's such a big shot. With his fine waist-coats and his shop—thinks he's better than the rest of us. They *all* think that!"

Max heard his mother say something in reply. He didn't hear what she'd said, but a moment later his father was off again.

"Well, he hasn't got a *car*, has he? So he can't be as great as he wants you to think. Shows you what they're like, all of them. Making out they're one thing while underneath, they're another thing completely. Liars, the lot of them. Sneaky, nasty, dirty, rotten—"

"Oh, do please STOP!"

There was a moment of silence. Max could hardly believe it. His mother never spoke back to his father—but she had this time. Max edged closer to the kitchen.

"I know what he is. I know how you feel about them. But he's the father of our son's best friend," his mother was saying. "Can't we just leave them be for now?"

His father was talking about Mr. Grunberg? Max couldn't understand. He must have gotten the wrong end of the stick. Everybody loved Leo's father. He was none of the things that his father had just said.

Either way, the ranting seemed to have stopped, so it was safe to go in.

Max softly pushed the kitchen door open.

His father was in front of him, his face red with rage. "Come in properly if you're coming in!" he yelled at Max. "Don't tiptoe in like a scared mouse. Enter the room like a man! And sort your hair out. Where is your parting?"

Max's mother crossed the kitchen to stand by his side. "Leave the boy alone," she said. "It's not his fault."

"What's not my fault?" Max asked.

His mother put a hand on his arm. "Nothing. Come on. Let's have lunch. You can do your hair afterward."

"Can I do it later?" he asked. "I'm going back out to play after lunch."

"Play?" his father burst in. "Who with?"

"Leo and Elsa," Max replied.

His father's face turned an even deeper shade of red. "Do you not have any other friends?" he asked. "Are they the only ones you can play with?"

What was Max to say? No. He *didn't* have any other friends. But he didn't want to admit that to his father and be a disappointment to him yet again. Besides, even if Max had had a hundred other friends, he'd still choose to play with Leo and Elsa. "What's so wrong with them?" he asked.

"What's so wrong with them? I'll tell you what's so wrong with them. They're—"

"NO!"

Max's mother broke in so sternly, it made Max jump.

"*No?*" his father replied. "You say no to me?"

His mother held her husband's eyes as she lifted her chin. "The boy is eight years old."

Nearly nine, Max wanted to say, but it didn't feel like the right time to interrupt.

"He can play with whoever he wants to play with," his mother continued.

31

Max swallowed as he felt the air fizz and crackle between his parents. Eventually his father gave a short nod. "Very well," he said. "For now, he can. For now."

The three of them ate their lunch together in silence.

As Max chewed his food, his mind went over the same question, over and over. The question his mother had stopped his father from answering.

What was so wrong with Leo and Elsa?

1937

Elsa

Mutti and Vati tell me the news as soon as I get home from school.

I've only come home to change out of my school clothes before going back out to meet Leo and Max as usual. But my parents stop me the minute I come in, sit me down, and tell me.

No ifs, no buts, no arguing. It's happening.

I stumble to the bathroom and stand in front of the mirror, saying it out loud, trying to believe it. Trying to imagine saying it to the boys. I can't.

"Are you all right in there, Elsa?" Mutti asks from the other side of the door.

I wipe a tear from my eye; they won't stop falling. "Just a few more minutes, Mutti."

She gives me a hug before I go out to play with the boys. She knows how I'm feeling without me having to tell her. Of course she does. She feels the same way.

"It's for the best, Elsa, sweetheart," she says as she strokes my hair. "You understand, don't you?"

I nod. But I'm lying. I don't understand at all. All I know is that it isn't fair. But Mutti already looks so sad, and I can't bear to make her feel any worse. So I don't say anything.

I wheel my bicycle down the hallway, and Vati holds the front door open for me.

"One hour," he says. "Okay?" He's so strict nowadays. Sometimes I feel like I can't breathe.

"Okay, Vati," I agree, then I hop on my bike and cycle to the park to meet the boys.

The park is beautiful. The sun is shining and blossom is coming out on the trees. Pink leaves bloom all along the path to the green where we always meet. The boys are both there already. They're playing games with toy soldiers.

"I win!" Max shouts, shooting dead Leo's soldier and raising his hands in the air in victory as I arrive.

I lean my bike against a tree and go over to join them.

"Come on. Now that Elsa's here, let's play tag," Leo says. Before I have time to reply, he slaps Max on the arm, shouts "Tag!" and runs off.

"Not fair!" Max protests. "We hadn't even said we're playing yet."

"You're just complaining because I'm faster than you," Leo retorts over his shoulder as he runs.

"No, you're not," Max replies grumpily.

"Come on, then, catch me!"

Max takes a step toward Leo. Then he glances at me. A glint comes into his eye and he switches direction.

Before I know what's happening, he's grabbed me around my waist. "Tag, you're it!" he shouts.

"Let go of me, then!" I squeal.

Max still has his arms around me. "What if I don't want to?" he asks.

I push him away. "Then I'll tag you back," I say.

I can hear Leo creeping up behind us. I hold Max's eyes and silently count to five—long enough for Leo to think he's safe—and then I twirl round. "Tag!" I shout, grabbing Leo's sleeve as he swerves so that I fall onto the bench.

He flops down beside me.

"Okay, one tag each," I say. "That's enough."

Max is standing in front of us. "Let's go to the pond. I think there should be tadpoles in there by now."

Leo jumps up from the bench. "I bet there will be. There was a whole load of frog spawn last week."

Both of them walk over to pick up their bicycles.

"Boys," I say. "Wait."

"What's wrong?" Leo asks, looking back at me.

I take a breath. This is it.

"I . . . ," I begin. Something is clogging up my throat. I swallow and start again. "I've got something to tell you."

The boys stop and stare at me.

"What's wrong?" Max asks. "Are you ill?"

I shake my head.

"Has something happened to your parents or Otto?" Leo asks.

"It's nothing like that," I reply.

They walk back over, concern on their faces. Leo sits down beside me again while Max stays standing in front of us. "What is it, then?" Leo asks.

"We're leaving," I say simply.

"But we've only just got here," Leo says. "We don't have to go yet. Surely you've got time to come and see the frogs before we have to—"

"Leaving Vienna," I say, cutting him off.

Leo's mouth falls open.

"Careful, you'll catch flies," I say, trying to keep my voice light.

Max folds his arms. "Where are you going?" he asks. "Are you going on holiday? How long will you be gone?"

"We're going to Czechoslovakia," I say. "To live."

"To live?" the boys blurt out in one voice.

I nod. I don't trust myself to speak. As I look down at my lap, a tear falls onto my dress. I swipe the back of my hand across my eyes. I don't want the boys to see that I'm crying.

Leo takes my hand in his. "For good?" he asks.

I nod again.

"You're leaving Vienna forever?" Max asks. His voice is husky. "But why?"

A funny feeling snakes through my insides before I reply. I don't want to say the words that Mutti and Vati told me. They sound silly. But I don't have any others to offer. I look up at Max. "My parents say it's not safe here anymore."

Max looks around at the park. "Not safe how?" He points at our bicycles. "Has anyone stolen our bicycles?" He waves an arm at the lanes behind us. "Is anyone acting suspiciously? How can it not be safe? What do your parents mean?" He sounds cross.

Leo isn't saying anything. He's stopped holding my hand, and his presence beside me seems to have hardened in some way.

"Not safe for *us*," I reply in a quiet voice.

"Us?" Max echoes.

I shake my head. "Not you," I say. Then I point at Leo and back at myself. "*Us*."

Max's forehead is creased as he frowns at me. "I don't understand."

I hold his dark eyes. A feeling of embarrassment washes over me as I reply.

"Because we're Jewish."

Max

Max burst out laughing.

Now he understood what was going on. They always did this to each other. The game was that you had to keep a straight face long enough to convince the other two of what you were saying. As soon as you knew they both believed you, you revealed the joke and won points for tricking them.

Elsa wasn't usually very good at the game. She wasn't like Max and Leo. She was a girl, after all. They were made of sugar and spice and all things nice. They didn't have it in them to play tricks.

Whenever she tried to trick them, she ended up giggling almost straightaway.

She wasn't giggling today, though.

Even so, she wasn't going to win any points off Max. What she'd just said was too ridiculous to believe even for one second.

He plonked himself down on the bench and leaned back. "You nearly had me there for a minute," he said.

"What do you mean?" Elsa asked. Her voice was all quiet and tinny. Oh, she was playing a good one today.

"Saying you were leaving Vienna. I *nearly* believed you."

"It's true," Elsa insisted. Her voice was getting smaller and smaller every time she spoke. "We're going on Saturday."

"But—but—" Max's thoughts were moving too fast for his words to keep pace. Something horrible was coming toward him from the back of his mind. A voice he didn't want to hear—a voice that sounded like his father's—was saying: *You know this, Max. You know it is true.*

He refused to listen. "But that's ridiculous," he insisted. "Your religion isn't a reason to leave Vienna!"

Elsa shrugged. "My parents say maybe it is."

Max clutched at the only straw he had left. "But you're not even properly Jewish! You don't even go to church!" he said.

"Synagogue," Leo mombled.

"Synagogue, then," Max went on. "Your mother doesn't wear a wig, your father doesn't wear one of those little hats. You don't pray differently. Even if your parents are right, how would anyone even *know* you are Jewish?"

"What about *my* family?" Leo asked Elsa. "We go to synagogue.

We say Shabbat prayers every Friday night. My parents haven't said it's dangerous."

Elsa spread her arms out in a helpless shrug. "Look, I don't know. I don't think it matters how much we pray or if we go to synagogue. We are Jewish, and my parents say that means we have to leave."

Max stared at his friend. For the first time, he noticed her eyes were red. Had she been crying? Was it really true? She was leaving? "And you're really going *this* Saturday?" he asked.

Elsa nodded. As she did, her eyes went all glassy.

"But your parents are mad!" Max looked at his other friend, desperate for one of them to stop that voice in the back of his mind from coming any closer. "Leo, tell her. What's being Jewish got to do with anything? How can being Jewish be *dangerous*?"

Leo was chewing on the side of his thumb. "I don't know," he said. "I suppose sometimes I think . . ." He shook his head and then turned to Elsa. "Did your parents really say that? It's dangerous?"

"They both said it," Elsa insisted. "I know it seems ridiculous, but they've got these stupid ideas in their heads and it's all decided. We're going, and there's nothing I can say to change their minds."

Max could feel something welling up inside him. It felt like a rock. A huge, bright red boulder, glowing with fire, pushing on his chest. His eyes stung with tears that were trying to get out, but he blinked over and over as hard as he could, trapping them inside.

Boys don't cry.

That's what his father always said. He'd said it only a few days ago. A bird had flown into the kitchen window, hitting it so hard that the bird had died instantly. Max had tried to revive it. He couldn't help the tears falling as he ran his fingers over its broken body.

"Do not cry over the death of a bird!" his father had yelled at him. "Boys do NOT cry. You hear me?"

Max had rubbed his fists against his eyes and wiped his runny nose on the back of his hand.

"Be a man," his father had growled as he snatched the bird away and threw it in the trash.

Be a man. Be a man. How many times had Max heard this from his father? He was not even ten years old yet. How was he meant to be something he wasn't?

Max sometimes felt that he could spend his whole life trying to be who his father wanted him to be, and he would still fail. No matter what he did, he would always fall short of expectations.

He couldn't bear the idea of things changing between him, Leo, and Elsa. Their friendship was the only part of his life where he didn't feel on the edge of things. Leo and Elsa were the only people who knew him as well as he knew himself. Being with them was the only place where he felt like he truly belonged. And now that was all going to change.

Boys don't cry. Boys don't cry.

Max clenched his fists and drove the tears away.

"This will be the last time I see you," Elsa said. Unlike Max, she wasn't trying to fight her tears, and they flowed freely down her face. That was all right, though. She was a girl. She was allowed to cry. Boys had to be stronger.

"In that case, this is the last chance to do something," Max found himself saying. The words were coming out of his mouth without even asking permission from his brain.

Elsa tilted her head toward him. "Do what?" she asked.

And before he could stop himself, Max leaned toward her. He said, "This." And then he pressed his lips on hers.

At first, her mouth was pursed up in shock. Then it softened and for two blissful seconds, their lips stayed together in a promise.

"Hey, you two!" Leo was speaking from somewhere outside of Max's bubble.

Max broke away from Elsa. He looked at them both. His best, most beloved friends.

And then, because he couldn't—he *wouldn't*—say goodbye, Max jumped up from the bench, grabbed his bicycle, and cycled away. His lips stung and his heart ached, but his mind contained only one happy thought as he pedaled as fast as he could: *I will marry Elsa one day.*

By the time he got home, he had almost convinced himself that it wasn't really happening. That Elsa's parents were wrong about it not being safe. They would realize it soon. And then of course they would stay in Vienna, and Leo, Max, and Elsa would laugh together at how silly they'd been.

Dangerous! What a thought. Of course it wasn't—

"Where have you been?"

The deep voice broke into Max's thoughts as the front door closed behind him.

Max looked up to see his father at the top of the stairs. He must have been working in his office and seen from the window that Max was coming down the street. He was nearly always in his office lately, when he wasn't out at meetings with important people from work. Either way, Max didn't see much of him nowadays, and Max knew better than to waste those precious moments making him wait for a reply.

"I've been in the park with my friends, Father," Max said.

His father took his glasses off and removed a handkerchief from his pocket to wipe the lenses as he came down the stairs. Putting his glasses back on, he stood in front of Max, eyeing him warily. "Which friends?" he asked.

"Leo and Elsa," Max replied. "My best friends."

His father nodded slowly. Then he turned to walk away. As he did, he spoke casually. "You are not to see them again," he said.

Max followed his father down the hall and into the kitchen. Had he heard correctly? His mother was in there, preparing dinner.

"Not to see my friends again?" he asked.

His father stopped walking. Max stopped too. So did his heart. His mother stopped what she was doing and looked at her husband.

Without turning, his father spoke again. This time his words were clipped and hard. "You make me repeat myself, Max? You really want to test my patience?"

45

"I . . . no. No, Father. I just—I thought I must have misunderstood."

Finally his father turned around. He bent down so that their eyes met. "I'll say it more clearly this time, shall I?" he asked. His mouth did something that might have been a smile if it weren't for the coldness in his eyes.

Max swallowed and nodded.

"Hermann, please," his mother said weakly.

Her husband ignored her. "You won't see Elsa again, and you won't see Leo again," he said to Max. "I forbid it. *Is that clear?*"

Max nodded even harder. "Yes, Father," he said.

Max's mother was standing in front of his father now, reaching out to him. "Hermann, stop," she begged.

He shook her off. "No. I've had enough. He needs to get this into his head, even if I have to spell it out to him."

"He's just a boy," she pleaded.

"Well, it's time he learned to be a man!" his father barked. Then he turned back to Max. "Your friendship with people like them is over. You hear me?"

Max stared at his father in horror. He didn't want to ask the question. He didn't want to hear the answer. He'd been running away from it all day, maybe for weeks, months—but it was there and it was coming toward him.

Before Max could stop himself, his mouth was forming the words. "People like who?"

His father spoke the word as if it were dirt in his mouth.

46

"Jews."

And with that, he turned away from his wife and son and walked to the table. Pulling out his chair, he unrolled a napkin and sat down for dinner, as though nothing had happened.

Max followed him without uttering another word.

He couldn't eat his dinner, though. Every time he tried to swallow, he felt he might be sick.

Leo

I sat at the kitchen table, trying to do my homework while Mama made challah—the bread we had every Friday night—but I couldn't concentrate. Elsa's words played over and over in my head, round and round and round like a record on Papa's gramophone.

Because we're Jewish.

Because we're Jewish.

Because we're Jewish.

In the park, I'd said that my parents hadn't told me it was dangerous—and it was true, they hadn't. Not in so many words. But still, something had held me back from laughing like Max had done. Something had stopped me from insisting it wasn't dangerous to be Jewish. Something to do with the tiny moments at home that I'd told myself I was imagining. Looks between my parents I'd pretended not to see. I couldn't put my finger on it, but if I thought about it, I knew that things had felt different recently.

Which was why I mostly didn't focus on it. Because if I did, my gut would tell me that perhaps Elsa was right.

"Leo, will you put your schoolbooks away now and help me set the table for Friday night dinner?" Mama called from the other side of the kitchen.

I shook myself. Chewing on the thoughts like a dog with a bone wasn't going to do any good. I closed the books I'd barely managed to read and put them into my schoolbag. "How can I help, Mama?"

"Fetch me the candlesticks and candles," she said. "And get the tablecloth, napkins, and cutlery out, please. Let's have the nice cutlery. I've invited Mr. and Mrs. Muller over for dinner."

"Really? How come?" I asked as I opened the drawer where we kept the fancy knives and forks.

"Their daughter is getting married next year. We're hoping they are going to ask your father to photograph the wedding, so we need to impress them."

I laughed as I pulled out the tablecloth from the drawer. "And you think fancy cutlery will help?" I asked.

Mama shrugged. "It can't hurt. Omama is coming too, so set an extra place for her, please."

As I reached into the drawer for the nice cutlery, which doubled as the drawer for odds and ends that had nowhere else to live, my hand fell on a piece of thin card. "What's this?" I asked.

49

I pulled it out. It was an envelope addressed to Mama and Papa, opened at the top with a sheet of paper inside.

Mama turned round. "Oh, that. Did you never see it?" she asked.

I shook my head. "What is it?"

"Open it. Have a look."

The letter was handwritten in German on personalized stationery. It had an address in England printed in swirly letters, with the words "Eric Stewart, Dental Practitioner" written in English above it.

The name was familiar, but I couldn't place it until I read the letter. It was very short and the German was clumsy, but the meaning was clear enough.

To dear Mr. and Mrs. Grunberg,
Thank you for the wonderful day we have not forgotten. We very much enjoy our time in Vienna more because of you. And of course, your lovely son and fantastic cake!
With best wishes,
Eric and Aileen

"The couple from the Ferris wheel!" I exclaimed just as Papa was coming into the kitchen. "That was nice of them to thank us."

"It certainly was," Papa said. He held out a hand, and I passed the letter and envelope to him. He read it over, then placed the letter back into the envelope. "Here, put it back where you found it," he said, handing it to me.

"Why have we kept it?" I asked, putting the letter back in the drawer as Papa had told me.

Mama wiped her hands on her apron as she smiled at Papa. "Because your father is a sentimental old fool," she said softly.

Papa smiled, but it wasn't his usual big, boisterous smile that brought a whole room to life. It was more like a flickering candle in the dark. "We keep it because we need to cherish reminders of sweet days and lovely people," he said, slipping an arm around Mama's waist as she leaned her head on his shoulder. "Especially in these times."

For a moment, none of us said anything. I wondered whether to tell them about what Elsa had said, but I was worried that if I said the words out loud, that would be the thing to make them real. If I didn't repeat what she'd said, if I didn't think about it, maybe I could still tell myself it might turn out not to be true.

Before I had made my mind up whether to say anything or not, the moment passed.

Papa shook himself and pulled his watch out of his pocket. "Right, the Mullers will be here soon. How about I open a bottle of fine wine for Shabbat?" He winked at Mama. "And maybe a brandy beforehand, to loosen us up?"

He put a record on the gramophone, and as he hummed along to the music and poured drinks and opened the wine and covered

51

the challah with a cloth so it would be ready for dinner, and as Mama tapped her feet as she cooked, the normality of it all made my heart settle back to its usual rate.

There was nothing to worry about. There was no danger. Of course there was no danger. Finally the knot that had been tied around my stomach since the afternoon started to loosen.

I couldn't wait to tell Elsa she'd gotten it wrong. I smiled as I imagined her, Max, and me meeting up at the weekend. How Max and I would tease Elsa about saying something so silly.

How we would all laugh at the idea that any of us might be in danger.

EARLY 1938

Elsa

I miss Leo and Max. I miss them terribly.

Missing them is the worst thing about living in Prague.

If I'm completely honest, it's the *only* bad thing. Everything else is actually quite good. I feel disloyal to the boys even thinking that, but it's true.

Since we moved, Mutti has started smiling again. Vati sings and whistles. He's got work again. Nothing big—he's doing odd jobs for people—but now that the word is getting around, he has quite a few clients. We can afford to eat without worrying. We even talk and joke while we're having dinner together, just like we used to.

School is hard because everyone talks a bit differently here. Some talk Czech; others speak in German. Mostly I can follow, but even when I do, my accent is different and that makes me want to keep quiet. So I don't join in with the other children that much, but I can mostly understand, and I'm learning quickly.

Otto seems to be getting on okay at school too. He's got a new group of friends who talk about cars and engines, so he's quite happy.

So, apart from missing Leo and Max, I'm glad we moved here. I'm happy.

Or at least I have been till this evening. I should have known it wouldn't last.

We're having dinner when Vati drops the bombshell.

"I'm going to join the army," he says. Just like that.

Mutti finishes her mouthful. Then slowly she puts down her knife and fork and turns to him. "Sorry?"

Vati won't look at her. "I'm joining the army," he says again. "Hitler's forces are coming, and we need to fight them."

"But we came here for safety," Mutti replies. Her voice is still calm. So is Vati's. I tell myself as long as they keep talking in a calm way, everything will be okay.

Vati puts down his cutlery and picks up his napkin. He wipes his mouth. "What is that safety worth if we don't fight to keep it?" he asks.

"But—"

"No buts." Vati cuts Mutti off. He never does that. "It's decided."

"Without talking to your family? Without asking *me*?" Mutti isn't sounding so calm now. Her voice is growing squeaky and high-pitched, and I can't kid myself any longer. Nothing about this feels okay anymore.

"Vati, when will you go?" Otto asks.

At last, Vati falters. He opens his mouth to reply. Then he turns to Mutti and closes his hand over hers. "I leave tomorrow," he says.

"Tomorrow?" I ask.

Vati nods.

I don't know what to say. I don't know what to do. I feel as if my insides are closing down. The room darkens around us as we sit there, stunned into silence.

And then Mutti pats Vati's hand and nods briskly before getting up and indicating for me to help gather the empty plates. "Well, you will need some food, then," she says. "Elsa and I will prepare your favorite biscuits. Otto, you are to shine your father's shoes, help him pack his case. Do whatever he asks. Yes?"

"Yes, Mutti," we reply together.

Mutti is piling plates in the sink, pulling pans out of cupboards, fetching flour and sugar and milk. "You will be the best-fed, best-dressed man leaving this city," she says. "And when you have done your part, you will come back to us, and we will try again to start this new life here. You hear me, Ernst? You hear me?"

She doesn't turn around, but I can tell she's crying because her voice has started to sound as if something is squeezing her throat.

Vati gets up from the table and goes across to Mutti. "Darling, stop," he says. "Come here." He pulls her to him and wraps his arms around her. She buries her face in his chest.

Vati looks across at me and Otto and indicates for us to join them. We run over to them, and Vati stretches his arms to go around us all.

"I will be back," he says. "I promise. I will be back, don't you ever doubt that, not even for one moment. We will get rid of this nasty Hitler man. Then we will get on with our lives. We will all be happy and we will be together. That's what is going to happen."

We cling to each other as if our lives depend on it. I tell myself, the harder I hold on, the more chance there will be of Vati's promise coming true.

"Now, then. Come on," he says, eventually pulling away. "Let's stop all this moping and get to work. You heard your mother. I'm not going anywhere without shiny shoes and the finest cookies. Tonight we are together and we will have a happy evening. I insist!"

And so, despite everything, we play music, we sing, we laugh, we talk, and we even dance, all through the night.

No one says as much, but we all know why we do it.

We need to fill our home with as many happy memories as we can, so they will last till Vati comes back to us.

Max

The headmaster had called a special assembly. He hardly ever did that.

Max could only remember it happening twice in his whole time at school. The first time was when Mrs. Ehrlich, the head of geography, died. Mr. Schmidt called all the pupils and teachers to the assembly hall, and everyone had to stand in silence and think about her for two minutes. All Max could think of was the time the hem of her dress had been stuck in her stocking for an entire lesson. He spent the whole two minutes trying so hard not to laugh that he almost did a pee in his pants.

The other time was when it had snowed so heavily that no one could see out the windows and everyone was brought into the assembly hall and told school was closing for a few days. That had been one of Max's favorite days *ever*. Everyone had played games in the assembly hall while they waited for their parents to pick them up, and Max had loved feeling like he was part of a big team. That they were all in it together. He'd happily have spent every day of winter shivering in a cold hall if it meant feeling like that again.

Mr. Schmidt had made sure everyone had plenty to eat and drink and even organized for extra blankets and coats when the pipes burst and the heating broke down completely.

That was Mr. Schmidt all over: kind, generous, thoughtful.

"I wonder what this is about," Leo said to Max as the boys shuffled into the hall with the rest of their class. Since Max's father had banned him from spending time with Leo, school was the only place they got to see each other. Max still hadn't told Leo the whole story. He'd just said his father had become more protective in recent months and didn't like him going out to play so much. Leo had never questioned him. Max assumed Leo had taken him at his word.

Since Elsa had left, things didn't feel the same anyway. Even if the boys could meet in the park, they'd only be conscious of the gap where Elsa should have been. And her empty seat between them at school had hurt Max's heart every time he saw it, till the teachers finally removed it and shuffled the desks around.

But at least Max and Leo could still see each other at school. Max's father couldn't stop them doing that.

"No idea," Max replied now. "Hopefully something good!"

"It's bound to be if it's Mr. Schmidt that's called us in," Leo said, pointing to the headmaster at the front of the hall.

"True."

They had all gathered in the hall now, and the teachers were looking around, putting their fingers on their lips and saying, "Shush!"

A couple of boys who were still talking got separated by the teachers. Max closed his mouth tightly and didn't say a word. He didn't want to run the risk of being moved away from Leo.

Finally the hall was silent. Mr. Schmidt craned his neck to look around, as if he were searching for something in particular. A couple of times, he did a quick nod of his head. Then he pulled a piece of paper from his pocket and quickly scanned it before clearing his throat. And then, in his big, booming headmaster's voice, he went straight to the point.

"If you hear your name, please stand."

Max glanced at Leo. Leo raised his eyebrows in a questioning way. It wasn't like Mr. Schmidt to be so abrupt.

"Heinz Bergman."

Everyone looked around to see who was being asked to stand. A young kid a few rows behind Max and Leo stood up.

"Samuel Adler."

Sam Adler was in their year! Leo and Max exchanged another look. What was going on? Leo shrugged, and then both boys turned back to Mr. Schmidt as Sam Adler stood up.

"Melanie Kronberger."

One of the older girls stood up.

It went on like that for a few minutes. A name. A pause while the girl or boy stood up. And on to the next name. No explanations from Mr. Schmidt. Was this a game? Max hoped so. Mr. Schmidt's games had been legendary ever since the snowy day.

There must have been ten or eleven kids standing when Mr. Schmidt said, "Leo Grunberg."

Leo turned to Max, his jaw open. "What have I done?" he whispered.

Max held his hands out in a wide *I don't know* kind of way. Then he grinned and put both of his thumbs up to encourage Leo as he shuffled from his cross-legged position to stand up with the others.

Max couldn't help feeling a tiny stab of jealousy. Leo always did better than Max did. Max had a sneaking suspicion that Leo was one of Mr. Schmidt's favorites, and this just confirmed it. Everyone being asked to stand up had probably won a prize or something.

But the flood of jealousy didn't last long. It was quickly overtaken by a feeling of guilt. Max should be pleased for Leo. They were best friends, after all, even if they had to keep it secret from Max's father now.

But still, Max sometimes felt invisible at school. He was one of the youngest in the year, one of the smallest among the boys, last to be picked for the sports teams, middle of the road with his marks. Sometimes it would be nice to be noticed and praised, like some of the other children. Like Leo.

Mr. Schmidt put his list back in his pocket and took a long breath as he waited for the assembly hall to be absolutely silent.

It seemed everyone in the hall held their breath while they waited.

And then Mr. Schmidt spoke, and Max would have bet the loose change in his trouser pocket that not a single person in the room would have guessed what he was about to say.

Leo

"**W**e here in this school, we citizens of Vienna, are overjoyed that the *Anschluss* has taken place," Mr. Schmidt began.

I'd heard of the *Anschluss*. I didn't know exactly what it was, but it had happened just this weekend. Mama and Papa had been talking about it in hushed whispers at home, and I knew it had something to do with the sudden appearance of soldiers on the streets. But I didn't understand what it could have to do with me, or with this assembly.

"We welcome our leader, the *Führer*, and we are proud to play our part in Greater Germany. We will obey all our new laws without hesitation. Indeed, we plan to set an example of how to behave, and we hope that other schools will learn from us and act similarly. From today, we have two important changes. The first is that, from this moment on, our school day will begin in a different way. You will no longer hear me over the loudspeaker, welcoming you and reminding you to leave your coats in the cloakroom and hurry to your classes. From now on, you will hear a new greeting from me."

Then he thrust his right arm forward, palm down, arm straight out, and shouted, *"Heil Hitler!"*

No one spoke, not even in a whisper.

Mr. Schmidt lowered his arm. "That is how we will *all* greet each other from now on," he said. He looked around the hall to make sure everyone was listening. I was starting to feel awkward standing up while almost everyone else was sitting. I wished he would get to the point so we could go back to class.

"The second important change is that we are going to show our dedication to the *Führer* and show our enemy their true place," he went on.

He raised a hand and pointed at each of us who were standing. "You dogs no longer have the same rights as everyone else in this school," he said.

I burst out laughing. I couldn't help myself. We weren't dogs! This must be one of Mr. Schmidt's games! A bunch of other kids laughed too. A ripple of giggles went through the hall.

Mr. Schmidt saw the laughing, and his face turned scarlet. "You Jews are lucky to be taught in this school at all!" he yelled, so loud I had to cover my ears. "From now on, you shall be treated like the lesser race you are! You will sit separately in lessons and assembly, at the back of the room." His gaze moved around the school hall. "The rest of you are not to interact with them. Jews are different

65

from us. They are dirty and inferior. For now, we have to put up with them in our school, but no one is to talk to them or play with them. You will pretend they do not even exist."

My feet were blocks of stone, rooted to the floor. I couldn't move. I still couldn't understand what was happening. Was it a joke?

If so, it was a really, really not funny kind of joke. And no one was laughing anymore.

The hall was completely silent.

"NO contact. Do I make myself clear?" Mr. Schmidt asked.

"Yes, Mr. Schmidt," the entire school replied. Even us Jews standing awkwardly among the rest. That's how conditioned we were to obey our headmaster.

I could still hardly believe what was happening, though.

I looked down at Max. I think a tiny bit of me was hoping he would flash me a grin and tell me to sit back down. Max would make me realize it had all been a mistake. That it was a joke, and the punch line was coming soon and then we'd all laugh. If so, I promised myself I would laugh the hardest.

Except, when I looked at him, Max didn't make me see that it was a mistake or a joke at all.

He made it a hundred times more real.

Max

Max didn't mean to do it. If you'd asked him the day before—even ten minutes before—he would have laughed in your face if you told him what he was about to do.

It didn't even feel like a decision that he made. It was pure instinct.

Max moved away from Leo.

Not a lot. Probably not even enough for most people to notice. An outside observer wouldn't have spotted a thing. But Leo wasn't most people; he was Max's best friend. Had he noticed?

Max's thoughts were spinning so hard they made him feel dizzy. What was happening? *Why* was it happening?

And why did it feel so familiar?

Almost as soon as he asked himself the question, Max knew the answer: Mr. Schmidt sounded like his father. Since the day he'd banned Max from playing with Leo and Elsa, Max's father still hadn't talked about it much at home. Mother wouldn't let him. But there had been a few times when Mr. Fischer hadn't managed to stop himself. He'd be reading the newspaper and would blurt out something that made Max itch with embarrassment: blaming Jews for everything that was wrong with the world, yelling about how much better off the country would be without them.

Max forced himself to switch off whenever it happened. Made himself believe that it was just his father, ranting. That he would get over it.

But he didn't. And now the headmaster seemed to have become infected with the same hatred.

Max could feel his best friend's eyes on him. He didn't dare look up, though. He couldn't bear to look into Leo's face and see what must be a world of hurt and fear in his eyes.

So, his face warm with shame, Max stared at the floor and shifted his body a tiny bit in the direction of the other children. The children who still belonged. A small part of his brain knew that he was letting his best friend down. But the bigger part had a question beating against it.

What if I'm next?

And so, he shuffled closer to a boy on his other side who he had never particularly noticed before, he stared at the floor, and he held his breath until the headmaster spoke again.

Leo

A memory darted into my mind out of nowhere.

My sixth birthday. Papa had taken us out for tea and cakes: me, Mama, and my grandparents. Throughout the meal, Papa had been jumpy and constantly looking at his watch as though he were expecting someone.

And then the door had opened and Papa had nudged me. "Here goes," he'd said.

I remember looking up at the most frightening thing I'd ever seen: a man with a big round face made of chalk, bright red lips that looked large enough to eat you alive, and eyes that could see into yours all the way down to your bones.

He was carrying a violin, and he came directly to our table, leaned toward me, and started playing a scratchy tune.

It was meant to have been a treat, but the strange man had

terrified me so much a warm liquid had spread down my trousers.

The shame had overwhelmed me.

I could still remember the strength of that feeling now. But as I stood there, in front of the whole school, being told I was an inferior being and feeling all the other children's eyes on me, I realized I had never known the real meaning of shame till this moment.

I tried to get Max to look up at me. I willed him to tell me this was a big mistake.

Please, Max. Make it all right.

He carried on staring at the floor.

"Come on, move! We haven't got all day," Mr. Schmidt shouted.

My shame deepening another notch, I turned away from my best friend and walked to the back of the hall.

Some of the kids still sitting on the floor stared at us with open mouths as if they couldn't believe what they were seeing. Others looked away, embarrassed and scared to be associated with the "dogs" that had been sent to the back. A few smiled at me as I passed; others touched my hand in sympathy. "I'm so sorry," a girl from the year above me whispered as I stepped over her legs.

"Chin up, it'll be all right," a boy I'd never spoken to in my life said to me from the end of a row as I passed him.

Their words meant nothing to me. Maybe if Max had said them, it would have helped. But these—they were empty words from children who just looked relieved it wasn't them at the end of the headmaster's pointed finger.

The twelve of us sat at the back of the hall for the rest of the assembly. And the back of each class for the rest of the day. We talked to each other a little. Not much. We had no words for what was happening to us.

Everyone else ignored us, as they had been told to do.

Even Max.

He wouldn't meet my eyes all day. We were due to have our last lesson with Mrs. Werner, but she stopped me at the door. Most of the other teachers had let us into the classes as long as we sat at the back and didn't speak. Mrs. Werner had always been strict and seemed to have used the new ruling to take her strictness to a new level. "No Jews," she said. "The rest of you, come in."

I stood and watched as my classmates filed past me and Mrs. Werner closed the door behind them.

And then I was left standing alone in an empty corridor, wondering what to do next.

Eventually I decided I might as well go home. I went to collect my coat and made my way to the front entrance. Even now, a tiny voice inside my head was still pleading for this all to be a big mistake. I could almost hear Mr. Schmidt's voice calling me back into school, apologizing for upsetting us. That was what Papa had done all those years ago when the clown terrified me. He'd apologized over and over, while Mama had wrapped me in her arms and stroked my hair.

I glanced behind me.

The corridor was empty. No one was going to call me back. No one was going to wrap me in their arms and apologize.

I turned back to the doors.

And then—

"Leo! Wait!"

I spun around. Max! At last! He hadn't deserted me after all. My heart swelled with relief.

He was breathless as he ran up to me.

"What are you doing here?" I asked.

"I asked Mrs. Werner if I could go to the toilet. I couldn't let you leave without saying goodbye." He shuffled from foot to foot. He always did that when he was finding something hard. "I'm sorry I turned away from you this morning," he said. "I'm sorry I haven't talked to you all day." His eyes filled with tears.

"I understand. You'd have gotten into trouble if you had."

"I know. But I'm sorry," Max said. "I'm sorry it's like this. And I know it'll be hard, but whatever happens, we'll find a way to stay friends."

I nodded. I couldn't speak. What could I say? Ask him how he thought we might do that now that we were banned from speaking to each other at school as well as outside of it?

Part of me wanted to ask him to tell me the real reason we didn't play together outside of school any longer. I knew in my gut that there was more to it than he had already told me.

But there were too many unspoken words between us, and I knew I couldn't say any of them. To do so would mean facing up to what all of this really meant. It would mean admitting that our promises of friendship forever were a lie—and I wasn't ready to do that. Not yet.

"Look, I—I've got to go." Max glanced furtively around. "Everything will be okay," he said.

"I'm sure it will," I replied. As he ran back to the classroom, I wondered if he believed it any more than I did.

I couldn't go home. The school day still hadn't ended, and I couldn't bear the thought of telling my parents what had happened and why I was home early. So I walked. I went to the park, to the canal, around the streets, walking and walking until my legs burned and my hands were so cold I could barely feel them.

Shame followed me around every corner, clinging to me like a dark shadow. A host of questions weren't far behind. What had happened today? *Why* had it happened? Who had made Mr. Schmidt behave like that? Had he always hated us and just pretended not to? And what about everywhere else? Other schools? Was it just our school where this had happened? Was it happening in Czechoslovakia? Was Elsa going through the same thing?

Since she'd left, we'd exchanged a few letters and cards. They got shorter each time. A few words on a piece of paper were no match for the reality of a best friend living a few streets away. But still, I thought about her every day.

For the first time since she'd left, I was glad she wasn't here. At least she was spared the horror of what had happened to me today.

Finally, after I'd wandered for a while, it was four o'clock and I could go home without having to answer any questions.

I made my way through the city, blowing on my hands to keep warm as I walked through the cobbled streets. As I neared

Stephansplatz, the main square in the middle of the city, I heard noise up ahead. I turned into the square and looked around. There was a crowd of people at the far end. What were they doing? It sounded like they were having a party. Pushing and jostling each other as they cheered and laughed.

So, rather than cutting across the center of the Stephansplatz to get home as I would normally do, I made my way to the far end of the square to see what was happening.

As I got closer, I recognized a few of Papa's friends among the crowd. Mr. Muller, Mr. Ferdinand, Mr. Weber. They were all there in their big coats and their black hats, laughing at something in the middle of the group. There seemed to be lots of soldiers in uniform too. Some were laughing, some were shouting.

It looked like fun. Just what I needed after today.

The crowd was too big to see through to the middle, so I wriggled between the men until I got to the front.

I would have given everything I had to change what I saw. I would have walked out of school in shame a hundred times over to make it not be real.

There were three men on the ground, kneeling in muddy puddles, arms out in front of them. It took a second for me to realize that they were scrubbing the pavement.

It took another second for me to see that one of the men was my father.

I felt like a cannonball had been hurled at my stomach. I

clutched my mouth. I could taste sick in my throat.

"Harder!" a man opposite shouted in a familiar voice. I looked up.

No. Surely not.

It was Mr. Fischer. Max's father.

He was wearing a uniform with a red armband on it. The armband had a shape I'd been seeing a lot lately. All the soldiers had them on their uniforms. It looked like an X, but each arm of the X was bent into a right angle. I knew what the shape was called.

A swastika.

I'd already suspected the swastika was a thing to be feared. Now, looking at the scene in front of me, I knew it for sure.

Mr. Fischer bent down toward Papa. A bit of spit sprayed from his mouth as he shouted again. "I said harder!"

My father looked up at him with pleading eyes from where he knelt in the puddle.

Papa.

The man everyone loved. The man who could make anyone smile, who would do anything for anyone.

My larger-than-life Papa, still in his smart suit and waistcoat, was kneeling in a puddle with a scrubbing brush in his hand.

"I cannot scrub harder, sir," he said.

Mr. Fischer took a step forward and stood in the puddle right next to Papa. "Maybe this will help," he said. And then he kicked my father in the stomach so hard that Papa fell forward, his face landing in the puddle.

"Papa!" I yelped as the crowd roared with laughter.

From the ground, Papa turned his head in my direction. His white, terrified eyes met mine. His lips moved silently. "GO!" he mouthed, before kneeling again and resuming his scrubbing.

The thought of leaving Papa there on his own horrified me. But the thought of staying terrified me more. So I did what he'd said and inched my way back out of the crowd.

I ran through the square and along the cobbled streets until I could no longer hear the crowd's baying and jeering.

And then, in the quiet of a deserted street, I leaned against a wall and retched, over and over, until my throat burned and my stomach cramped.

Even so, the pain was nothing compared to the ache in my heart.

Max

Max sat at the kitchen table with his homework. He'd been looking at the same page for over half an hour, but every time he read a line, his mind swam with the morning's events and he couldn't focus.

Sadness and confusion battled against each other inside his chest.

The strangest thing was that the day had continued like any other. The assembly had been dismissed, children had been sent back to classes, and everything had gone on as normal. As if twelve of their schoolmates hadn't been called dogs and separated from the rest of the school.

The sound of the front door closing made Max jump. His father was home early. Mr. Fischer came to the kitchen doorway.

"Come here," he said to his wife as he crossed the kitchen. She was at the sink preparing vegetables.

Max's mother wiped her hands on her apron and turned toward her husband. "You seem happy," she said as he took her hands in his and kissed her.

"I *am* happy," he said.

"Good day at work?"

"An excellent day," he said. "Very productive."

Mrs. Fischer looked down. "Your boots are covered in mud!" she exclaimed. "How did they get like that?"

Her husband waved a hand as if to swat a fly away. "Oh, it was nothing," he said. "Just some dirt that got in my way." He laughed as if sharing a private joke with himself. "Anyway," he went on. "I have good news. I have been promoted."

Max's mother clapped her hands. "Oh, that's wonderful!" she said. She turned to her son. "Max, darling. Isn't that wonderful?"

Max forced himself to smile. Even the effort of doing it made him feel like a traitor to his friend. "That's very good news, Father," he said.

"It is. Hitler has singled me out for a new role. I have been instrumental in strengthening his work here in Austria. I have shown an exemplary level of commitment and loyalty, and now he wants me to join the heart of the movement. I am to become a senior SS officer."

"What does that mean?" Max's mother asked.

Mr. Fischer smiled before replying. "It means we are moving to Munich," he said. "We leave next week."

Max tried to respond, but found that when he opened his mouth, no words came out. If this had been just a day earlier, he would have been devastated to be taken away from his home, from Leo, from everything he knew.

But now? Now he wasn't sure what he felt.

Maybe moving somewhere new and starting over would help take away the pain of knowing that his best friend was so near but he wasn't even allowed to talk to him. Maybe it would soothe the pain he still felt in the gaps where Elsa used to be.

Maybe it would help ease the guilt that had followed him all day like a heavy burden on his back.

It wasn't as if he could have done anything at school that morning. It wasn't Max who had humiliated Leo. It wasn't his fault. But still, he felt it. The unfairness of it. The fact that he hadn't even tried to speak up for his friend.

Why hadn't he? Would he, if he had the chance again?

Max didn't want to torture himself with questions. He wanted to run from them, run as fast as he could.

He could have a fresh start in Munich. Start again, maybe even make new friends.

They were leaving in a week. Max told himself he would talk to Leo before they left. And he told himself that he would find a way to keep his promise of friendship.

He told himself whatever he needed to hear—even if, somewhere down in the depths of his heart, he knew it was all a lie.

LATE 1938

Elsa

Our days are mostly the same as each other. The pattern is strangely comforting.

School; homework; help Mutti with dinner; sew or read together till the light fades; bed.

And through it all, try hard not to think about Vati.

As soon as he comes into my mind, the questions pile in with him: Where is he now? What is he doing? Is he safe? Is he even alive?

I don't have any answers, so I do my best to chase the questions away with routine and chores and helping Mutti.

Otto is doing the same. We don't talk about it, but I can tell. Only, instead of sewing and reading, Otto has become even more obsessed with fixing things. He has been taking woodworking at school and seems to spend every minute at home looking for anything made of wood that he can take apart and rebuild. Maybe mending *something* helps him cope with all the things in our lives that we *can't* fix.

This evening, as usual, we are trying to keep ourselves as busy as possible. I'm holding the end of an old dress while Mutti patches a hole in it. Otto is sitting on the floor with one of the kitchen stools. I watch him out of the corner of my eye, the concentration on his face—his narrowed eyes, his tongue poking out of the edge of his mouth—as he unscrews one of the legs and rubs it with sandpaper before tightening it back into place.

"That's better!" he says triumphantly as he turns the stool upward and sits on it.

Otto's wide smile makes Mutti laugh softly. "You're a good boy," she says. Reaching out to stroke my arm, she says, "What would I do without the pair of you?"

Otto puffs his chest out. "You'll never be without us, Mutti," he says.

He says it so somberly, it hurts my heart. My big brother trying so hard to be the man around the house and look after me and Mutti.

As we sew, I tell Mutti about my day. I'm fitting in well at school now. I've made a friend called Greta. Greta has always lived here in Prague, and she was assigned to help me out when I started school. She has dark, curly hair and green eyes that sparkle mischievously when she smiles. She smiles a *lot*, and laughs and dances and talks.

I've never met anyone like her before; being around her is like having a balloon that is always filled with air.

Last week she called me her best friend. I couldn't believe it. I thought she would have loads of best friends, but she said she's never liked anyone as much as she likes me.

I wanted to say the same back to her, but I stopped myself. I was worried it might be disloyal to Leo and Max. But secretly I liked it when she said it, and I think I'll tell her soon that she's my best friend too.

I'll write and tell the boys. I have sent a few letters, but we are so busy here that it's hard to remember to send them every week. They'd understand. I know they will.

My friendship with Greta is completely different from my friendship with them. With Leo and Max, it was all about playing, being outside, having fun, going on adventures. Greta and I mostly spend our time talking.

We talk about all the important things, like:

Do we prefer cats or dogs? Dogs for me, cats for Greta.

What is our favorite color? Pink for Greta, yellow for me.

What will we be when we grow up? Greta will be a writer; I will be an inventor. Greta says that she doesn't know any girls who have become inventors. I nearly change my mind and tell her I'll be a teacher instead. I don't want to fall out with her, as she's my only friend here in Prague. But she tells me it's fine. I can be an inventor if I want to be an inventor.

"You can be anything you want to be!" she declares, flashing me one of her infectious smiles.

The next question: Who will we marry? I tell her about Max and Leo. Greta says that she will marry Leo and I will marry Max. And then she throws her head back and laughs, like she does at least twenty times a day.

And my favorite question: How long will we be friends? We agree on this one. For always.

That's how I know that Greta is officially one of my best friends. I've decided. I'm going to tell her tomorrow. She'll be so pleased. I imagine her meeting Leo and Max. I hope that one day that might actually happen.

That will be the best day ever.

Max

Everything was different from the very first day of their new lives in Munich.

Max watched from the window of the big black car as they traveled through the streets. Vienna was grand and beautiful, but Munich had a different feel. Vienna might have palaces and opera houses and a river running through it, but Munich felt more serious, somehow. The kind of place where important work would get done.

Mr. Fischer tapped on the window and instructed the driver to stop.

He got out of the car and came round the side to open the door for his wife. "We're home," he said with a flourish as the three of them stepped out in front of a huge gray building with a row of pillars stretching along the length of it.

Max's jaw dropped open. "This is our new house?" he asked.

His father burst out laughing. A rare occurrence, and Max was pleased to have made him laugh. "Not the whole building," he said. "We have an apartment." He pointed up to the top floor. "But I think you will like it. It is the penthouse. We have a balcony with views across Munich."

Max's mother clapped her hands. "I shall feel like royalty," she said, her voice high-pitched with excitement.

"My darling, that is exactly what we are now," her husband replied. "We are Hitler's royalty. This is how you are rewarded for rising above the others and giving your life to the regime as I have done these past years. This is what I have earned for us."

Max thought for a moment of all the times in Vienna when his mother had stood up to his father, told him to go gently on Max or challenged him on his views. It seemed that a fine apartment in Munich and a promise of the best things in life were enough to make her put all that behind her and welcome the new start—just like Max welcomed it.

Max's father clicked his fingers, snapping him out of his thoughts. "Max. Come and help with the luggage."

Max ran to the back of the car, where the driver had already unloaded bags and cases onto the pavement. Max could feel his father watching him and, as always, was desperate to show he wasn't a weak boy, so he went straight for the biggest case.

He couldn't even lift it off the ground.

His father shook his head and said, "Just my luck that I have a little squirt for a son."

Max gritted his teeth and stared at the ground, trying to hide his reddening cheeks. Then he shook the words away. He was used to his father saying things like that; it didn't mean anything.

"Come on, Max, shape up," his father prodded him. "We don't want to be here all day."

Max picked up a couple of smaller bags and carried them into the building, then all the way up the winding marble staircase.

Mr. Fischer unlocked a door on the top floor and opened it with a flourish. "Ta-da!"

Max followed his parents into the grandest room he had ever seen. The lounge area was bigger than their whole apartment in Vienna had been. Along one side was a cabinet chock-full of books. On the other, a long wooden table with ornately carved legs. In the center of the room were two large settees and an armchair in between. His mother had been right, it really did look like the kind of place royalty would live.

But the best part of it was the windows—and what was outside them. Max ran across the room to look out the biggest window. It was taller than he was, and opened like a door. It looked out over the big square they'd driven through earlier.

"Here," his father said, coming up behind Max and opening the door. Outside was a small balcony; just big enough for the three of them.

They stood together, looking out. Max's eyes were wide as he stared down at the square below them. Lots of people were bustling about: mostly soldiers in uniforms like his father's. Grand buildings lined the square. The grandest of them all was opposite. In the middle of the building was a tall spire that reached halfway to the clouds.

"What's that?" Max asked, pointing.

"That is the town hall. I will be attending many meetings there." Max's father checked his watch. "Come back here at midday or five p.m. and watch those figures below the clock," he said, pointing at what looked like giant toys sitting in an opening in the tower. "They do an extraordinary dance."

Max couldn't even imagine such a thing. He couldn't wait to see it.

"Come, let me show you the rest of the apartment."

As they explored, it seemed to Max that every room held a delight, a surprise, something ten times grander than he had ever seen. Max's bedroom was about three times bigger than his room in Vienna.

He couldn't stop smiling all day.

The next morning, Max barely touched his breakfast. He was starting his new school that day, and his stomach was tying itself into knots. He wasn't sure if it was nerves or excitement; probably a bit of both. His chest twisted and tightened when he imagined school without either Leo or Elsa beside him. But then he reminded himself that this was his chance to have a fresh start. He could reinvent himself in Munich. He didn't have to be the boy who only had two friends. He could be anyone he wanted to be. Maybe even someone his father could be proud of.

His father gave him some stiff words of advice before he left for school. "Don't stand out. Don't speak out. Do exactly what your teachers tell you and copy the other boys if you are unsure."

Max nodded. "Yes, Father," he said.

"And *don't* let me down."

"I won't, I promise, Father."

Just an hour later, Max was in his new classroom waiting for the teacher to arrive. As soon as the man walked into the room, every boy instantly stood to attention. Max jumped out of his seat to do the same.

The teacher stood in front of the class and flung his right arm out in front of him, hand in the air, palm facing down, and shouted, "*Heil Hitler!*"

Instantly every child in the room did the same in reply. Max's teachers at his old school had been instructed to do the same thing just before he'd left, so he had become used to the new greeting. But here the response was so instant, so instinctive, that Max was a moment behind everyone else.

The teacher noticed that Max had been out of step with the others and stared him in the eye. "New boy," he said.

"Yes, sir," Max said, hoping that no one could hear the nervous wobble in his voice.

"You will be quicker next time," the teacher said. "The *Führer* does not stand for tardiness."

Max nodded fiercely. "Yes, sir. Sorry, sir," he said.

Then they were seated and the school day began.

Max got used to his new school over the coming weeks. It couldn't have been more different from his old school. In Vienna, school had been fun. At least, it always had been when he'd been able to spend time with Elsa and Leo. He got an ache in his chest when he thought about them. He wanted to write to them, wanted to tell them all about his new life—but somehow he always came up with an excuse not to. For one thing, his father would be furious if he found out about it, and Max was keener than ever not to upset him. For another, Max was so busy with his schoolwork he barely had time.

But there was another reason too, and Max didn't want to admit to this one—even to himself.

He was starting to feel part of school life in a way he had never before. Every day, his number one aim was to do what his father had said on the first day.

Don't stand out. Don't speak out. Do exactly what your teachers tell you and copy the other boys if you are unsure.

And it was working. Max *didn't* stand out. He wasn't the one singled out for taunts and laughter. He was becoming one of the crowd, and he liked it.

He soon discovered he liked having strict rules, too. The regimented day made things straightforward.

You were given orders; you followed them. You didn't have to think for yourself; you just had to do exactly what you were told, and you would be fine. The only attention you got was praise and respect. And it was addictive. The more Max got these things, the more he craved them. And the less he thought about his old friends.

Within weeks, Max made sure he was always one of the first to stand to attention when a teacher walked into the room. He shouted his "*Heil Hitler!*" salute as loud as anyone else. He worked as hard as he had ever worked in his young life. And his reward was that he quickly became part of the fold.

That was all he wanted. It was all he had ever wanted. Only now, the fold wasn't a gang of three friends where he felt safe from everything. Now he was *part* of everything, a cog in something bigger and more powerful than himself.

And if there were times when teachers said things that made him itch under his skin, he wouldn't show it. He knew better than that.

When they had lessons about how to be a good Nazi, or why the German race was superior to all others, Max didn't think about the ones who might be left behind. He comforted himself in the knowledge that he was one of the lucky ones. His father was a Nazi soldier. His family was part of the superior race.

He began to feel proud.

When their teachers told them how important it was to rid themselves of the scourge of the Jewish enemy, how the Jews were filthy, inferior, disgusting creatures, Max kept his face as still and impassive as he possibly could.

He didn't question them. *Don't stand out.*

He didn't argue. *Don't speak out.*

He didn't tell them his old friends were Jewish. *Be like the other boys.*

But secretly, in his bedroom at night, when no one was around, Max would sometimes let himself think about Leo and Elsa. Still, he couldn't bring himself to write to them. Now more than ever. He would feel like every word he sent them was a lie. And anyway, he hadn't heard from them either, so he didn't need to feel guilty.

But he let himself have small moments to think about them, and to smile at the memory of their games and laughs together.

He would take out the photo that he still kept hidden in a drawer. He would still smile as he remembered that moment: looking down at Vienna from high in the air, laughing all day.

And then the questions would come. Were Leo and Elsa *really* the enemy? Were they the people he had to hate? Could there be a mistake of some sort?

He knew he could never ask these questions aloud, and so, with an ache in his chest, he would put the photo away, and to help get rid of the painful thoughts, he would stand in front of his mirror and recite his school's motto over and over until there was nothing else in his mind.

"One people, one empire, one leader!"

"One people, one empire, one leader!"

"One people, one empire, one leader!"

Leo

I made a list of things I was no longer allowed to do. I carried it with me everywhere in case I forgot. I'd seen what happened to people who forgot.

Like Papa, when I'd seen him in the square. Except Papa hadn't even had time to remember. He'd barely had a day to learn the new rules before he was punished for breaking them.

We never talked about that day. Neither of us even acknowledged it had happened. Instead we both pretended that our eyes hadn't met when he was kneeling on the ground, that he hadn't urged me to run away so I wouldn't face a similar fate, that I hadn't known any different when he came home and told Mama that he had slipped and fallen in the rain.

Sometimes I reran the events in my mind, trying to find even a sliver of possibility that I had misunderstood what I'd seen. I made up alternative versions and tried to convince myself they were real.

Papa had been playing a game with his friends. They were taking it in turns to be in charge. He had fallen, like he said to Mama. Mr. Muller and Mr. Weber and the others weren't laughing and jeering *at* him, but *with* him. They *must* have been: those men were his friends.

Even Mr. Fischer used to be friendly with him. He didn't really kick Papa in the stomach. He can't have. He must have been doing something else.

But as the days went by and the friends stopped coming for dinner, and the clients started going elsewhere, and Papa grew so withdrawn he rarely spoke and no longer smiled, it became harder and harder to convince myself that they had been playing a game.

And when his beautiful studio window that had always been filled with photographs of smiling people had "JEW" daubed across it in red paint that dripped down the window like blood, I stopped trying to force my mind to lie to itself.

I knew what I had seen and why my father and the other men on the ground with him had been singled out by that crowd. And I knew it could happen again—to him, to me, to any other Jew in the city.

That was when I made my list of all the new laws that I needed to remember. Here's what it said:

I am no longer allowed to . . .

Go to school. (Except the Jewish school I now have to
attend. I am still allowed to go there.)
Go to the park. (It's not as much fun without Elsa and
Max anyway, so this one is okay, I suppose.)
Go to restaurants. (Just as well Mama is such a good cook.)
Go to public swimming pools. (Boo! I love swimming.)·
Ride bicycles. (This is the WORST. I love my bike.)
Say "*Heil Hitler.*" (I don't mind this one. I secretly hate
Hitler. He is the one who told the men to beat up Papa, so
I don't want to "*Heil*" him or any of his horrible men.)
Join the Hitler Youth. (See above.)
Marry someone who is not Jewish. (This one might be
useful one day, as it means that Elsa will have to marry me
because she won't be allowed to marry Max.)

I checked my list constantly. Every day, we would hear of someone else who had broken the laws. They were beaten or imprisoned
or taken away, no one knew where. My life became a daily promise
that I would not become one of those people.

So I memorized the new laws and followed them without question
or exception. And every evening I opened the drawer where I kept the
list. I read through every point; then I folded the list back up and put
it away, offering silent thanks that it had kept me safe for another day.

Elsa

I t's an evening like all the others. Mutti gently hums as she sews. I sit at the kitchen table with my schoolbooks. Otto is fixing something in his bedroom.

It is all quite peaceful. Other than Vati not being here, life in Prague is still going well. I had a letter from Leo last week, telling me about the situation in Vienna. It sounds terrible. I know for sure now that we did the right thing to move. I just hope things quickly get back to normal there so Leo can get on with his life too.

A knock at the door shakes me out of my thoughts.

No one ever knocks at the front door, and my heart knocks along with it. Mutti's eyes are wide. Her face drains of color. "Stay here!" she hisses as she puts her sewing down beside her and gets up.

"I'm coming with you," I say, and I follow her into the hall. Otto is at the top of the stairs.

Mutti stands in the entryway. She takes a breath and then, in a shaky voice, asks, "Who is it?"

The house is silent for a second, and then a familiar voice calls back from outside the door. "It's me! Are you going to let me in?"

Vati!

The catch is pulled aside and the door flung open. Otto darts down the stairs at the speed of light. I run the length of the hall, and there he is. Vati! He's back!

I throw myself at him before he has even closed the door behind him. Otto jumps up and down next to me like a puppy desperate for his turn.

Vati laughs. "Let me at least get in the house," he says as he puts down his bags and turns to Mutti.

Her face is streaked with tears. "You came back," she whispers hoarsely as he takes her in his arms.

"I told you I would," he replies. "I promised all of you we would be together again."

"Is the fighting all over?" Otto asks.

"I hope so," Vati replies.

"Did you win?"

Vati opens his arms in a wide shrug. "That question is too complicated for a simple answer. For now, I think so. We'll see."

Mutti steps back and takes his hand. "Come, let's go in the kitchen." She turns to me and Otto. "I'll make hot chocolate for us all. Let your father sit by the fire and get warm before you hound him with questions."

We follow Mutti into the kitchen. I fetch milk for the chocolate, and Otto stokes the fire while Vati takes off his coat and boots before coming to join us.

"You are home for good, aren't you, Vati?" I ask as I come over to sit on the edge of his chair. "You're not going back?"

"I don't plan on going anywhere," he says.

Mutti brings him a steaming cup of hot, frothy chocolate. He kisses her as he takes the cup. "Just as I like it," he says.

"So what's happened?" Mutti asks once we've all had a drink. "How come you are back?"

"I don't know all the details," Vati says. "They don't exactly share state secrets with us, but it seems there's been a deal of some sort."

"What kind of deal?" Otto asks.

"One made by the politicians and lawmakers," Vati says. "Hitler has signed an agreement with Britain, Italy, and France promising that he'll leave Czechoslovakia alone."

"Leave us alone?" Mutti asks.

"They've said Hitler can have some territory to the west as long as he promises not to invade the rest of Czechoslovakia."

"And he agreed to that?" Mutti asks.

"He did!" Vati says. He smiles. "It seems war has been avoided and we've all been sent home!"

I don't understand most of what Vati is saying. I understand the last bit, though, and that's all I need to know.

Vati is home, and our family is back together again. Whatever danger there was, it's over.

Otto and I are allowed to stay up late to celebrate. Just as well, as I'm far too happy to go to sleep anytime soon.

Max

The best thing about life in Munich was, without doubt, Max's new circle of friends. The Hitler Youth had changed his life. In fact, it would have been fair to say the Hitler Youth *was* his life.

Gone were the days when Max would huddle with his two friends on the fringes of everything, playing tag in the park, making up their own games, laughing at their own jokes.

He was part of something much bigger than that now. No, not just *part* of something; he was at the *center* of things. Max lived for the weekends, when he would dress in his crisp new uniform and join the boys in the square. They would march in rows, as if they were a single mechanism. Their *"Heil Hitler!"* salutes were shouted in perfect unison.

They weren't just a group of friends. They weren't just a team. They were a unit with one voice, one mind, one aim: to be perfect Nazis.

At age ten, Max was in the junior section, called the German Youth. He couldn't join the senior ranks of the Hitler Youth till he was fourteen, but Max didn't care. Fourteen was still such a long time away, he didn't even think about it. Being in the German Youth still meant he felt part of something bigger, something important, and his friends felt the same way.

After marching, the boys would go to the Hofgarten park to train. They ran relay races, played tug-of-war, and learned how to light campfires and make knives from twigs.

Max trained harder than any of the other boys. He ran faster, pulled more fiercely, cheered on his teammates louder. Soon he was one of the first to be picked for a team. He was the one slapped on the back the most times at the end of the races. He could barely recall the days when he had been forgotten, picked last, teased for being weak.

He always went home bursting with so much pleasure he sometimes thought he might pop like an overfilled balloon.

It was on a day like this that something happened to put a tiny dint in Max's bubble.

He and his friends were marching home from the park. They had been dismissed for the day, so they didn't *have* to march, but they did anyway because they enjoyed it.

They marched down the road four abreast, almost taking over the whole width of the pavement.

A man coming toward them had to dodge out of their way. As the man hopped off the pavement, one of the boys called out, "Smelly Jew!" Another held a hand out in front of his face, pretending to extend his nose out into a huge hook shape.

The other boys laughed. Max forced himself to laugh too. Inside, though, he got an uncomfortable wriggly feeling. Saying horrible things about Jews was the only thing he didn't really like about his new life.

And the things they said—Max still wasn't convinced they were even true. His best friends had been Jewish—but they didn't have huge noses and they didn't smell.

So Max did what he always did in these situations. He forced his mind through the mental hoops he had constructed over the time they had lived in Munich. He told himself that if Leo and Elsa weren't stinky and didn't have big noses and weren't nasty and evil, that meant they couldn't really be Jewish. Maybe they had mistakenly *believed* they were. Maybe Max had thought they had told him they were Jewish but actually *he'd* gotten it wrong and they were something else altogether.

Before long, Max had convinced himself that Leo and Elsa weren't Jewish at all. They *couldn't* have been. And if they weren't Jewish, then Max didn't have a problem.

If they weren't Jewish, then he didn't need to question himself every time someone said something about the Jews. If they weren't

Jewish, maybe he could even write to them, rekindle their friendship, tell them all about his new life and the Hitler Youth. They would be pleased to know he was so happy.

That night at dinner Max took all his courage in his hands, cleared his throat, and in the most polite voice he could muster said, "Father, could I ask you a question, please?"

His father finished chewing, swallowed his mouthful, and replied, "Of course."

Max's heart was thumping like the bass drum the boys banged at band practice. And then the words came out in a rush.

"Father, I've been thinking about my old friends from Vienna, Leo and Elsa. I think we might have been wrong about them, and I was wondering if I might perhaps be allowed to write to Leo."

Max's father carefully placed his knife and fork on his plate. Then he wiped his mouth, put his napkin back in its holder, and turned to his wife. "Excuse us for a moment, darling," he said. Then he got up from his chair and indicated for Max to do the same.

"Your room, now," he said, and Max followed his father to his bedroom.

Once inside, his father softly closed the door. When he turned back to look at Max, his face was bright red, and his eyes were tiny black holes.

Max swallowed.

"How dare you," his father hissed. "After all we have done for you, the sacrifices we have made, the work I do for the cause of our great country and our great leader, and this is how you repay me?"

"Father, I just—"

"DON'T interrupt when I am talking!" His words felt like a slap to the side of Max's face.

"Your mother has spent half the day making us a nice dinner, and you spoil it by mentioning JEWS! What are you thinking?"

"I—I—I wondered if perhaps there was a mistake," Max stammered. "That maybe they aren't Jewish after all."

"Not Jewish? They looked like Jews, they smelled like Jews, they skulked around like Jews, they preyed on the rest of us. Of *course* they're Jewish!"

Max wanted to argue. He wanted to say that his friends didn't do any of those things. But he knew better than to argue with his father, especially when he was this angry.

"And what are Jews?" Max's father asked.

Max hesitated. Terrified of saying the wrong thing, he said nothing.

"They are pigs," his father said through his teeth. "They are *worse* than pigs. They are scum. Vermin. Filth. They are rats."

"Yes, Father."

"Say it. Jews are scum. Jews are rats. Jews are filth."

Max tried to get the words out, but when he tried to speak, the taste of bile in his mouth stopped him.

"Say it!" his father ordered.

"Jews are scum. Jews are rats. Jews are filth," Max mumbled quickly.

"Louder."

Max swallowed down the bile in his throat and tried to speak louder. "Jews are scum. Jews are rats. Jews are filth."

"Louder!"

Max raised his voice. "Jews are scum. Jews are rats. Jews are filth."

"Louder!"

Max shouted. "Jews are scum! Jews are rats! Jews are filth!" He could feel a tear snaking into the corner of each eye.

"Again!"

"Jews are scum! Jews are rats! Jews are filth!"

Max's father stalked across the room and fiddled with the window catch. Max quickly swiped away the disloyal tears that had squeezed out of his eyes. He couldn't let his father see him cry. He wouldn't let that happen.

His father flung the window open. "Come here. Tell the world!" he said. "As loud as you can. Over and over."

Max ran to the window. He filled his lungs with air, and then he poured every bit of guilt, shame, anger, and confusion into his words as he screamed at the top of his voice: "Jews are scum! Jews are rats! Jews are filth! Jews are scum! Jews are rats! Jews are filth! Jews are scum! Jews are rats! Jews are filth!"

By the time his father indicated for him to stop, Max's forehead was coated in sweat, his heart was pounding like a train, and his legs were so weak he thought he would faint.

His father closed the window. "Good. Don't *ever* forget that," he said. "And you are *never* to speak of those filthy Jewish children in this house again."

"I won't, Father. I promise." Max knew it was true. He would never allow himself to be put through this after today. He would do anything to avoid making his father so angry again. He would never again doubt what Leo and Elsa were. He would never even think about contacting them. He would banish them from his mind.

His father looked at him for a long time without speaking. Then in a quiet voice, he said, "Are you ready to put your words into action?"

Max would have agreed to anything his father suggested in that moment. "Yes, sir."

"All right, then. You'll join us tonight. It's a big night. An important night. I am giving you an opportunity to prove to me that you aren't completely useless and to show me that you are ready to play your part."

"I'll show you," Max said fervently. "I promise. I won't let you down."

"Good. Now, let's go and finish our meal."

Later that night, Max and his father left the house in the dark and headed to the city's Jewish quarter, with a growing army of men joining them at every corner.

Armed with bricks, stones, and a heart that had begun to beat to the rhythm of rage, Max was determined to honor his promise.

Leo

What was that?

A crashing sound had woken me, and I sat bolt upright in my bed. I held my breath and listened for a moment. Nothing. It must have been a cat jumping off a roof. They did that all the time.

I was about to lie back down when I heard it again.

CRASH!

This time there was no mistaking the sound: breaking glass. It sounded like it was quite far away.

I crept out of my bed and tiptoed across my bedroom.

CRASH!

This one was closer. I edged to the window and, kneeling on the floor, lifted a corner of my curtain so I could look out without being seen.

A gang of men were walking down the street. Some dressed in black with heavy boots and big coats, others in the SS uniforms and helmets I'd grown used to seeing on the streets every day.

I had never seen them at night before. They looked like my worst nightmares, multiplied by ten. They looked like an army of darkness coming directly for me. My heart beat so hard I had to clutch my chest to make sure it stayed inside my body.

As the men came closer, I could see they all had armfuls of bricks or large sticks. I watched as they stopped outside a shop doorway halfway up the street. One of them gave a nod to the others and then—

CRASH!

The men threw bricks through the window. Then they slapped each other on the back and moved on. They were getting closer to our house. They didn't stop at every shop window. Why not?

As soon as I asked myself the question, I knew the answer: they were targeting the shops owned by Jewish people.

Suddenly Mama was outside my door. "Leo. *Liebe.* Darling boy," she whispered.

I dropped the curtain and crept to my door. She opened it and reached out for me. "Come," she whispered. "Stay down."

Together we crawled across the landing and crept downstairs and into the hall. Mama silently beckoned me to the door under the stairs. "In here," she said, gesturing for me to crawl into the cupboard.

A split second's memory opened in my mind. Playing hide-and-seek with Elsa and Max. Elsa had hidden in here behind the boxes at the back. Max and I hadn't been able to find her and had given up in the end.

I hoped the men outside would do the same.

We were about to crawl inside when I heard the back door softly open. My heart stopped with fear—until a familiar face appeared at the end of the hall.

"Papa!" I breathed with relief. Then I noticed that his face was cut and bleeding and he was limping. His coat was torn and his trousers ripped at both knees.

"We were—at—the—synagogue," he said, his words coming out in breathless raspy bursts. "Praying. Praying for an end to this. They came. They came to our place of worship. They are destroying every part of us."

Mama pulled him toward her and hugged him hard. I could see Papa's shoulders shaking as he sobbed in her arms.

I had never seen him cry. Not once in my whole life.

"Hush, my love," Mama whispered in Papa's ear as she stroked his hair. "They will never destroy us. Never."

She beckoned to me. "Leo, fetch the medicine box. Quickly. Then come back."

I ran to the kitchen and grabbed the box from a drawer. Mama ushered me and Papa into the cupboard under the stairs.

"I'll fix you up in here," she said to Papa as she followed us into the darkness.

As she tended to Papa's wounds, I sat in the pitch black, praying for the night to be over and pretending I couldn't hear my father's sobs over the sound of breaking glass.

At some point, we must have fallen asleep.

When I woke, my head was in Mama's lap and she was resting against Papa's shoulder.

We dragged ourselves out of the cupboard and stretched to straighten our bodies out.

"Come on, let's eat." Mama went into the kitchen to prepare breakfast.

I looked at Papa. "How can we think of eating?" I asked.

He put his hand on my shoulder and replied, "How can we not? We must stay strong, Leo. We must do everything we can to hold on to our dignity. All right?"

I bit my lip and silently dared the tears to show themselves. They didn't. Then I nodded.

"Come here," Papa said. He pulled me close, and I flung my arms around him. I breathed in the comfort of him: his worn jumper and the scratchiness of his unshaved chin.

We had only just sat down to eat when there was a knock at the door.

My instinct was to run back to the cupboard under the stairs. Papa stood up.

"No. Please." Mama reached out to grab his arm.

"What do you want us to do, darling? Hide in a cupboard forever?"

She let go, and Papa went to answer the door.

I heard familiar voices in the hall. It was Papa's friends. Maybe they had come to check if we were okay.

The relief didn't last long.

Papa's face was gray when he came back into the kitchen, flanked by two of the men, a third one behind him. The last time I'd seen all three men was in the square, when they'd been laughing and pointing at Papa.

"I have to go," Papa said to us.

"Go?" Mama asked, getting up and crossing the kitchen to join him. "Go where?"

"You shouldn't ask, Mrs. Grunberg," Mr. Weber said. He'd been friends with my father as long as I could remember. He'd sat with us at this very table. Eaten Mama's cakes, drunk Papa's wine. He'd worn a kippah on his head while my father said prayers over our bread.

"I shouldn't ask where you are taking my husband?" Mama replied, her voice as sharp as her best kitchen knives.

Mr. Ferdinand was on Papa's other side. "He needs to come to the police station," he said.

Mama clapped a hand to her face. "You are arresting him?"

The third man standing behind Papa stepped forward. It was Mr. Muller. "If he comes with us, they will leave you and Leo alone," he said.

Mama stared at Mr. Muller. "How long have you been friends?" she hissed. "How much has my husband done for you?"

Mr. Muller held his hands out in a helpless shrug. "We don't make the rules, Mrs. Grunberg," he said, as formal as a police officer. "But we have to take him now."

Papa turned to the men. "Just give me five minutes."

The men looked at each other. Then Mr. Weber nodded. "Five minutes. We'll be in the hall."

The second they left, Mama ran to Papa. He wrapped his arms around her, beckoning me to join them. The three of us stood huddled together in silence for a few moments in the middle of the kitchen. I wanted to stop time, turn those five minutes into forever.

Papa pulled away eventually. He knelt down and cupped my chin in his hand. "I'm going so I can keep you safe," he said. "You heard them. If they have me, they will leave you and Mama alone."

"But what if they don't?" I asked. "What if they come for us, too?"

He shook his head. "It's me they want. You are the man of the house now. You look after your mother. You do everything you can to help her. You hear me? You promise me?"

"Yes, Papa. Of course I promise."

He pulled me in for one last hug before standing up again. He spoke quickly, in a low, rough voice. "Listen," he said. "We don't have much time. I wasn't going to talk to you about this till I had good news, but it's too late for that now. You have to take over from me."

"Take over what?" Mama whispered back.

"Arrangements for getting out of the country. I've been looking into it, and you must continue my work and get away from here."

"What? You want us to leave our city, our home? Without you?"

"You must go," Papa insisted. "While they have me, it will buy you some time. But you need to work quickly."

"We're not going anywhere without you," Mama said.

Papa looked fiercely at her, then at me. "You have to," he said. "I will come back for you, I promise. I will find you, wherever you are. But you can't stay here. Listen. The paperwork is in my office. Find it and pick up from where I left off."

"What about Omama?" I asked.

Papa almost smiled. "I have tried to persuade her, but she says she is too old. She is too stubborn. She will not leave, and I cannot change her mind. She has her friends, and I hope they will look after each other. But, Leo, while you're still here, you make sure to visit her as often as you can." His voice broke as he added, "And do not leave without saying goodbye to her and making sure she is all right. You hear me?"

I nodded. My throat hurt too much to speak.

"It's time to leave, Mr. Grunberg," one of the men called from the hall.

"You will get out of this country," Papa said to us both, his voice a hoarse croak. "Promise me."

Eventually we nodded at him. "We promise," Mama and I said in unison.

And then he leaned in for one last wordless hug before he turned, straightened the collar of his bloodstained shirt, and went to join the men.

115

As the front door closed behind them, I bit my lip so hard I could taste blood. I would not cry. I would not give them that. I was the man of the house now. I had to look after Mama. I had to finish what Papa had started and help Mama to get us out of there. I had to keep my promise.

For the second time in less than twelve hours, I stood by the window, lifting a corner of the curtain to look out.

I watched Papa walk down the street to the police station, flanked by three men he used to call his friends.

His crime: being Jewish.

1939

Elsa

Hitler has taken Czechoslovakia.

It's all anyone talks about at school. What will this mean for the people of Prague? What will happen to our families, to our schooling, to us?

The tension takes over my body. I try my hardest not to think about how bad things were before we left Vienna. So bad that my parents made us leave our whole lives behind. Will we have to do that again? Will I lose Greta now, in addition to Leo and Max?

Leo tells me things in his letters about how his life is now. Or he did, anyway. I haven't heard from him in a while. Life is bad over there. Very, very bad. I can't help thinking that everything he has described is what is now in store for us here.

Did we do all of this, uproot our lives, only to put the horrors off by a year and not escape them at all?

I'm in math when the headmaster sends a message for all teachers to read out to their classes. We're told that afternoon lessons are canceled so that our teachers can learn about the changes that are coming. There are going to be new laws, and they need to understand how to implement them in the school.

The others cheer at the news that we will have the afternoon off. My throat feels too gummed up to cheer. Still, I'm glad for a chance to get away from all the talking about what's going on.

Greta isn't in my class for math, but I hope I can find her when we break for lunch, and then we can spend the free afternoon together. I try to rush out to catch her, but my teacher, Miss Jansky, stops me. "I'm sorry, Elsa," she says, placing her hand on my arm.

"Sorry? What for, miss?" I ask.

She doesn't reply. She just shakes her head. Then she squeezes my arm and gives me a sad kind of smile. I'm starting to feel a bit uncomfortable and I'm not sure how to respond.

"You coming?" Frida, one of my classmates, is waiting at the door.

"Go on," Miss Jansky says. "Take care, Elsa."

I'm relieved to get away from the awkward moment.

"Some of us are going into the city after school," Frida says to me. "To see what's going on with Hitler's army! Want to join us?"

I think about what Mutti and Vati have said to me recently. They don't like me going anywhere without telling them where I'll be. They've started being all protective again, like they were in Vienna before we left. And Hitler was the man Vati went to fight! I don't want anything to do with him! Just his name scares me. But I don't want to say any of this to the girls and sound like a baby.

After Vati came home from the army last year, we thought things were going to be great. We thought all our troubles were over. But things have been tough lately. Vati's work has dropped off. No one seems to be offering him contracts, and Mutti's been quieter again. They haven't talked about any of it with me and Otto, but I still feel it. There's something different in the air.

I've got a tiny voice inside me wondering if maybe our troubles haven't even begun.

But I know I can't say any of this to the others. Luckily, Greta is beside me before I can reply to Frida.

"We've got plans," she says quickly. "We'll see you tomorrow."

The other girls shrug and move off without us.

"*Do* we have plans?" I ask Greta as the girls walk away.

"No, of course not," she replies.

"Why did you say we did?" I insist, even though I'm grateful that she did.

"Because it's dangerous in the city," she says.

"Dangerous?" I ask. I can't stop myself. Every nerve ending in my body jangles with tension, and I know I shouldn't push it. I don't want to say it out loud. I don't want Greta to say it either. But if I don't, I'm scared the tension inside me will burst out and break me into pieces.

"You know it as well as I do. We're Jewish," she whispers urgently. "It's not the same for us. Not anymore."

And finally I have to face the truth that has been lurking inside me all along. The cold words hang heavy in the air around us. The words that are so similar to those I said to Leo and Max two years ago.

I want to argue; I want to laugh; I want to tell her she is being silly.

But in the end I don't do any of those things because the truth is, I know that Greta is right. It's not the same for us. *Nothing* is the same for us now.

Leo

I ran to the door to greet Mama. She'd been out all morning. She greeted me with a simple shake of her head, and my heart deflated.

It was the same every day now. She would go from embassy to embassy, from one administrative task to the next, from one crushing disappointment to yet another.

I went with her sometimes. We would stand in long lines, edging slowly forward for hours on end, unable to leave the line to get something to eat or drink or even visit the toilet, for fear that we would lose our place. Finally, after many hours, we would get to the front. Mama would hold out the papers we had been told we needed in order to leave Austria, and every single time our hopes would be dashed. There was always some reason why they wouldn't sign the papers, something we had done wrong, some tiny detail that made them send us away empty-handed.

One time, the official behind the desk didn't even look up at us. We had stood in line from eight in the morning, and it was now a minute before five.

"We are closed," he said. "Come back tomorrow."

"Please, sir, I have waited all day," Mama replied. "There is still one minute. I just need your signature. Surely you have time to do that for me? I am begging you."

The man slowly lifted his head. He looked Mama in the eyes. For a second, I let myself believe he would do what she asked. Why wouldn't he? It was the simplest of requests.

"I am a slow writer," he replied with a cruel laugh. "Now get out and do not make me repeat myself or you will regret it."

He went back to his paperwork, and we shuffled out of the office and walked home in silence.

Another time, Mama had managed to get one set of papers signed. Then she was told to go to another building to get a second set stamped. I went with her again. This time the line was shorter. We were in the final line before lunchtime. Our spirits were high, and I remember Mama even smiling as she handed over the required documentation. This was it. We would be a step closer to leaving the country.

But when she handed over the paperwork, instead of simply stamping it and sending us away, the man behind the desk shook his head. "You have done this wrong," he said. "You are meant to get it stamped *first*. Then you get the other section signed. I cannot accept this." He ripped the papers up in front of our eyes. "Start again," he said as he casually dropped them into the bin beside him.

"I can't go through it again," Mama said to me now. It was more than four months since Papa had been taken away, and we were no closer to leaving Vienna than we'd been that day. "What's the point?"

"Mama, we can't give up," I tried to argue. It wasn't even about following Papa's urgent plea for us to leave anymore. We knew even without him there that he was right; we had to go. Every day told us that Austria was no longer a country for us. The daily taunts, the restrictions on our movement, the curfews—it was no way to live, and Mama knew it as well as I did.

"I can't do it," Mama said. "They act like cats toying with a helpless mouse for their own entertainment. I won't put myself in that position again. I refuse to give them the satisfaction. And anyway, even if we manage to get these documents signed, we still don't have all we need, and we never will."

"Why is that, Mama?"

"Because it is not enough for them that we leave everything behind—our home, our possessions, my *husband*! We have to have a sponsor in a country we want to go to. Someone to vouch for us, give us a home, a job, assure the Nazis that they are rid of us for good." She looked at me, her eyes dark and heavy-lidded. "Leo, my darling," she said softly. "We don't know anyone in another country. There is nobody waiting to help us."

125

"But, Mama, we have to keep trying," I insisted.

She softly put her finger over my lips. "I'm finished," she said. "No more. We will brave things out, and your father will soon be home, and then we will all be together and get through this as a family. It can't get any worse than it is now. Just hold tight and we will get through it."

"Okay, Mama," I said with a deep sigh. What choice did I have?

In the silence that followed, I heard an envelope land on the mat by the front door. I went to get it. I recognized the writing.

"Papa!"

"Look, see, something good!" Mama said as she picked it up and tore the envelope open. Each month we had received a letter from Papa. This was the fourth one. I lived for those letters.

We certainly didn't have much else to live for these days.

"Come, let's get into my bed and tuck ourselves under the blanket to read it," Mama said. Snuggling under the blanket together was one of the upsides of the fact that we didn't have enough money to put the heating on. We could hardly afford anything since Mama had been forced to sell Papa's photography studio for a fraction of its value. The Nazi Aryanization laws meant Jews were barely allowed to own anything nowadays. We were lucky we still had our home.

Mama had had to hand over all her jewelry, too. Luckily, the day the Nazi soldiers came for it, she'd already had an idea what they were coming for. People in our neighborhood had been whispering about it for weeks. Just the night before they came, she had taken off her wedding ring and sewn it into the hem of an old blanket.

It was the only piece of jewelry she still owned, but she never dared even take it out to look at, let alone wear it.

For me, the most treasured possessions I had were these letters from Papa.

I jumped into bed and pulled the blanket around us. Mama unfolded Papa's letter, and we read it together.

My dear wife and son,
   I am well and everything is fine. They feed us and look after us so well you would hardly think I was in prison! I have made friends here and I work hard each day. The guards are friendly. You must not worry about me at all. I will see you soon.
   Leo, I hope that you are looking after all my old photographs. Remember what I always say about photography? That a picture paints a hundred words. Remember that! You know I am telling the truth! And that's why you must always remember to do everything I tell you! You are the man of the house now.
   I love you both with all my heart, and I will see you very soon. Please don't forget to check on Omama, and send her my love too.
   Papa

Mama smiled as she folded the letter. She held it to her mouth and kissed it.

It was so rare to see her smile nowadays that I didn't want to ruin the moment, but something about Papa's letter was bothering me.

"Mama, can I see it?" I asked.

"Of course. Put it with the others when you've finished."

She handed the letter to me and I read it again.

Then I realized what it was. Papa's words about taking photographs weren't right.

Remember what I always say about photography? That a picture paints a hundred words.

That *wasn't* what he always said. He always said a picture paints a *thousand* words.

Had he forgotten that? Surely he couldn't have. Papa would never forget something so important to him. Something he said to me over and over again.

But then why say it?

I read on. *You know I am telling the truth!*

My heart thudded as though it were on springs as I realized: Papa was talking in code! By lying about the phrase, he was trying to say he *wasn't* telling me the truth about the other things in the letter! I reread his words. All the things he said about how good everything was—he was lying. He obviously didn't want Mama to worry, but he was sending me a message, I was sure of it.

And that's why you must always remember to do everything I tell you!

There was only one thing he had told me to do: get out of Vienna.

Which meant I had to think harder. I had to find a way to help Mama be stronger. We *had* to leave.

As I folded the letter up and took it to the special drawer in Mama's room where she kept the other letters, I had a sudden memory of doing something similar. A drawer with something special in it.

What was I remembering? Was it a dream or a real memory? It was getting harder every day to hold on to the good memories, so I was about to dismiss it as an illusion. But then, just thinking about memories brought that wonderful day into my mind. My ninth birthday. The memory of that day brought more pain than joy nowadays, so mostly I didn't think about it.

Except, for some reason, it was tugging at me now.

And then I realized why.

The letter! The letter from the Stewarts!

I hurled myself down the stairs and ran into the kitchen. *Please still be there, please still be there, please—*

Yes! There it was! Still tucked at the back of the fancy cutlery drawer.

I charged back upstairs. Breathless with hope and excitement, I ran into Mama's bedroom. "Mama," I said. "We mustn't give up."

"What? Give up what?"

"We *have* to get out of Austria."

"Leo, please, not this again. I've told you—"

"I know. And . . ." I paused. *Should I tell her about Papa's secret message?* No. If he had wanted her to know, he wouldn't have sent it in code. I was the man of the house now, like he'd said. I had to find a way to make this happen.

I sat on the bed and talked quickly. "Let's just give it one more go," I said. "We'll get up before the dawn breaks. We will be first in every line. We will smile and listen and do everything perfectly, and we will get the papers in order. We'll take every step together."

Mama sighed. "But, Leo, I told you, even if we do all that, we still come to a dead end. We still have no one to vouch for us. We have nowhere to go!"

I thrust the letter out to her. "Yes we do," I said firmly.

"What's this?" She took the letter from me and opened it. Then she laughed softly. Sadly. "The English couple from your birthday years ago," she said.

"They might do it," I said. "They might help us."

Mama shook her head. "Darling, a ride at the fair and a piece of cake do not equate to what we would be asking of them."

I drew a slow breath and puffed out my chest. "Mama," I said. "They are our last hope. They are our *only* hope. We have to try."

Mama held my eyes for a long while. As she did, I realized what was making her so reluctant. It wasn't that she *wanted* to give up.

It was that she couldn't bear to let herself hope, only to have that hope dashed again.

Finally she nodded. "Okay," she said. "I will write to them tonight."

I threw my arms around her. "Thank you, Mama," I said, kissing her cheek.

I wished I could tell Papa that I had a plan. Even if it failed, at least we were trying to do something.

That had to be better than letting the Nazis take everything without us even putting up a fight.

Max

Max woke before his alarm went off. He was out of bed even before the sun had risen, before his parents got up.

He made his bed and, still in his pajamas, crept into the kitchen, where his mother had laid out his pressed uniform the night before. The first thing he did was check that the creases in his shirt and shorts were all in the right places. Next he pulled out his boots from under the table and inspected them.

"Max, what are you doing?" His mother stood in the kitchen doorway, yawning as she pulled her dressing gown close around her and glanced at the clock. "It's not even six yet."

Max held up a boot. "I wanted to shine my shoes, Mother."

She laughed. "Again? Surely you shone them well enough last night?"

Max's father appeared behind her. "Leave the boy alone," he

said, coming past her into the kitchen. "He's doing a good job."

Max stared down at his boots so his father wouldn't see his flushed face. If he knew how much joy Max got from his occasional snippets of praise, he might give them out even less frequently.

As Max grabbed a cloth and gave his boots one last shine, his father came to sit at the table. "What time are they picking you up?" he asked.

"At eight, Father," Max replied, barely managing to keep the excitement out of his voice.

He was going on his first Hitler Youth weekend. A whole weekend with his friends: two days of races, games, making fires, camping out in the woods, toasting bread on an open bonfire. But mostly it would be two days where they got to act like soldiers. Marching in their ranks, their feet stamping in perfect time, their *"Heil Hitler!"* salutes synchronized to a T. These were the things that made Max's heart sing. The feeling of being a small cog in a large, perfect machine was like nothing he had ever felt before, and he couldn't get enough of it.

The weekend was even better than Max could have dreamed. Whenever it was time to line up, Max was at the front. When they came to pick teams, Max was elected captain of his. When they had to carry logs across a river, Max picked the heaviest log and waded across the deepest part. When the other boys made jokes about Jews, Max laughed the hardest, and when they thrust their hands in the air and shouted *"Heil Hitler!"* Max shouted the loudest.

So it was an easy decision for the leaders that, when medals were given out at the end of the weekend, Max was declared "Best Boy in Camp."

His teammates carried him high on their shoulders, calling out his name as they gave him three cheers.

Max felt that he owned the whole forest, the city, the world.

For a brief second, he remembered feeling something similar once before. Looking down at a city as if he were king of all he could see.

Then it came to him: Vienna. The Riesenrad. That day at the top of the Ferris wheel with Leo and Elsa.

The memory gave him a strange sensation in his chest. Not a good sensation. Not a comfortable one. One that seemed at odds with the boy he was now. And he couldn't afford to let anything stop him from being the boy he was now. He had far too much to lose. So, before the memory could take hold, he shook it away and dragged his thoughts back to the present moment. It was safer there.

Leo

I t's here! Mama, it's here!"

I ran up the stairs and into Mama's bedroom. Sitting on the side of her bed, I shook her as gently as my excitement would let me. "Mama, wake up!" I insisted.

Mama opened her eyes. "Whatever is the matter, Leo? Has something happened?" she asked as she yawned and rubbed her eyes.

I thrust the letter in front of her. "Look at the postmark, Mama. It's from England!"

The word worked like smelling salts. Mama was upright in a second. "Give it to me. Let me see."

I passed her the envelope, and she studied it as if it were a precious object.

To us, it was.

Then she pursed her lips and placed the letter carefully on the bed. "Coffee first," she said.

"But, Mama!"

"Coffee first," she insisted. "There is no need to run headlong into this. I want to be awake first. I will need all the energy I can summon if I am to deal with the disappointment of a refusal."

Mama was right, and she had reminded me of the most likely outcome. It had happened to almost everyone we knew. Every Jewish family I knew had only one aim nowadays: get out of Austria any way possible.

A friend of Mama's who had managed to hide enough money to pay for an ad in a British newspaper had even advertised herself as a domestic servant. She showed us the ad last week.

"Austrian woman, highly qualified teacher, seeks work as domestic maid in an English home. Please help. Desperate."

She had so far had no replies. No takers. Just another Jew that no one wanted.

So yes, Mama was right. It was best to put off the moment when our last hope—our *only* hope—would be gone.

We managed to hold it off for half an hour while Mama drank her coffee and I washed in the bathroom sink. We never used the shower anymore. Our hot water had long been cut off, and a quick wash in the sink was more bearable than standing under a stream of cold water.

Then we sat together at the kitchen table, the letter between us.

Mama nodded, as though making a deal with herself. "Open it," she said, handing the letter to me.

"Me?"

"I can't bear to read the words myself. I will know from your face what they say."

I could almost hear Papa's voice. *You're the man of the house now.* It made me bold. "Okay," I said, and I slid my finger along the edge and pulled the envelope open.

Elsa

Mutti and Vati have been whispering again. Like they did just before we left Vienna. They think Otto and I don't know about it. They think we are asleep in our beds, but we're not. We're crouched at the top of the stairs, straining our ears to catch an occasional word or phrase and trying to piece them together.

"Just as bad . . ."

"Never have left . . ."

"Won't come to that . . ."

"Desert our own children . . ."

"Transport . . ."

"No, never. Don't ask me that . . ."

Our imaginations are working overtime, and finally Otto and I decide that the truth can't be as bad as the images we are conjuring in our minds. So we go to confront our parents, together.

"Hey, kids, you should be in bed," Vati says, jumping up from the table as we step into the kitchen, both in nightgowns, both silent, as we haven't worked out quite what it is that we want to say.

The truth is, we don't *want* to say it at all. We just know that whatever "it" is, we can't keep pretending it isn't there.

"It's way past your bedtime," Mutti says. "What are you doing down here?"

"We can't sleep," Otto says.

Mutti smiles across at us. "Want me to read you a bedtime story like I used to?" she asks.

I shake my head. "No thanks, Mutti."

"Hot chocolate?" Vati asks.

"We want some answers," Otto says firmly.

Before either of our parents can respond, I find myself blurting out my fears, hot tears springing into my eyes as I do. "Are you leaving us?" I ask.

Mutti stares at me. Vati opens his mouth to speak, but nothing comes out.

"You are!" Otto bursts out. "You're leaving us! You're abandoning us!"

Mutti gets up from the table and reaches an arm out toward me and another to Otto. I run to her and let her comfort me with one of her warm hugs. I breathe her in and hold my breath. If I can keep my breath in until she replies, then she will tell me no, they will never leave us. Otto stands firm, waiting for answers.

"Of course we aren't abandoning you," Vati says. I let my breath out with relief. But there's something about his voice that doesn't assure me quite as much as I'd hoped.

"We've heard you talking," Otto says. "We think you are planning something."

"Something you don't want us to know about," I add, leaning away from Mutti so I can watch her face.

Mutti glances across at Vati, and I see them exchange something: a quick nod of agreement.

"You're right, we have been talking about something," Vati says. His voice is so serious, and for a moment I want to take it back. I want to go back upstairs, get into bed, pretend I never heard the whispers. Whatever it is, I don't want to know.

"Come. Both of you," Vati continues. "Sit with us at the table. I'll make you that hot chocolate and then we will talk. It's time we told you about our plans."

Even the heat from my hot chocolate can't stop my hands from shaking as we wait for them to tell us what's going on.

Leo

I stared at the letter. I couldn't speak.

Mama reached out to take me in her arms. "Leo, darling, it's all right. We'll be okay. We will find a way."

I shook my head. Holding out the letter, I found my voice. "They said yes, Mama," I said. "The Stewarts said yes!"

"What?" Mama took the letter from me. She read aloud. "'We will do what you ask. Of course we help you. Your kindness and generous day we always remember. Please tell exactly what you need and we do it immediately. Our best regard, Aileen and Eric Stewart.'"

Mama stared at me. Finally I let my face break into a smile. "They are going to help us," I said in a whisper. "I can't believe it."

Mama smiled back at me—but I could see there was something bothering her. I didn't need to ask what it was. I felt the same way.

"Papa will find us," I told her. "He will join us as soon as he can."

Mama nodded, tight-lipped, but didn't say anything. I thought of the coded note Papa had sent to me. I had to be the strong one. "And Omama will give us her blessing," I added. "She will never leave here, she has told us so many times. But, Mama, *we* have to go." I put an arm around Mama's shoulders. "Papa wants us to go; he *needs* us to go."

Mama slumped against me. "I know, Leo, my love. It's just . . ." Her sentence trailed away.

"It's hard," I finished for her. "I know. It's *really* hard. But Papa would be even more unhappy if he thought we had stayed here when we had a chance to leave. It's an awful choice, but this is the best of the two horrible options."

Mama leaned away from me. Looking into my eyes, she put her palm against my face and stroked my cheek with her thumb. "When did you grow into such a sensible young man?" she asked.

When I had to, I thought.

I didn't say that, though. Instead I kissed her cheek and whispered, "I love you, Mama."

"I love you more, my darling boy," she said. Then she took a breath and seemed to gather herself into action. "Come on, then. Let's take the letter to the authorities and see what hoops they make us jump through this time."

We wrapped up in our biggest coats and thickest gloves and hats and began the trail of embassies and offices and administrative buildings that we had become used to visiting. We armed ourselves for another day of standing out in the cold, and for the usual rejections, laughter, and scorn.

But they didn't come.

The day ended with something we never thought we would receive: a visa.

Elsa

I rub my eyes and stare at my parents. I must have heard them wrong. I *must* have. Half of me wants to ask them to repeat what they've just told us. The other half is terrified of hearing the words again.

"You can't be serious," Otto says before I have decided which way to go. "You're sending us away? This has to be some kind of a joke, right?"

Vati turns toward my brother. "Do we look like we are joking, Otto?" he asks, his voice husky and dark.

"But—but things aren't really so bad, are they?" I ask.

"How bad do you want them to get, Elsa?" Vati replies. "It's not enough that neither you nor Otto is allowed to join the youth groups with all the other children? Not enough that I have no work, that you are not allowed to walk in the park, ride your bicycles, go swimming! Not enough that our friends are disappearing on a daily basis?"

Mutti puts her hand on his arm. "Darling, go gently on the children. They don't need to think about all this."

"But, Stella, that's just it. They *do* need to think about all this. We have to face what is happening."

"We *are* facing it," Mutti replies calmly. "I am with you on this decision. But still, we don't need to ram it down their throats."

Vati lets out a breath. "Very well," he says. "But the decision is made. We just have to sit tight and wait till we are given our date. But it will be soon."

"Soon? Like, weeks away?" Otto asks.

"Days, more likely," Vati confesses.

"Days?" I croak.

Mutti is crying openly now. "My babies. Believe me, if we thought we had any other options, we would take them."

"But why can't you come with us?" Otto asks. My big brother, the one who always tries so hard to be tough and strong and capable, sounds as scared as me.

"They won't let us," Vati replies. "We are not allowed out of the country. But you children have a chance. And your mother and I will not sit here and let the chance go by without reaching out to grab it."

Mutti kneels in front of Otto and me. She takes our hands. "You are the most important things in our lives," she says. "There is nothing that I care about as much as you."

"Then why are you sending us away?" I ask. My throat hurts and I can barely get the words out.

"Because we want you to live," Vati says simply.

"We're living now," I argue weakly. "Can't we just carry on as we are?" I think about the last time we went through this, leaving my two best friends. In Prague I have only one true friend. I can't bear the thought of saying goodbye to Greta.

"It will only be for a short while," Mutti says. "Just till all of this passes over. You'll be back in no time."

"Can I tell Greta?" I ask.

"No!" Vati is firm. "We can't let anyone know that you are going. We all carry on as normal until I get word of the date you will leave. When that comes, we will all travel to the train station after nightfall. We have papers for you already. It is all organized. You will go to Holland and then get a boat to England. You will be looked after every step of the way. There are good people out there who will make sure you are safe."

Mutti tries to smile at us both. "And then, when everyone is sick and tired of Hitler and it is safe to come back home, we will collect you," she says. I know she is trying her hardest to convince us that everything will be fine. And because I can't bear to see her trying so hard to hide her sadness, I give in.

"Okay," I say. "We'll do it."

Otto half shrugs, half nods. "We understand," he says.

But I know he's lying just like I am. We all are. How could any of us understand that our lives are really in so much danger that Otto and I have to travel to another country, one where our parents aren't even allowed to follow?

I'll do it. I'll go. But I refuse to understand—because that would mean accepting the reality of what our lives have become. And I'm not prepared to do that.

Leo

I couldn't stop staring at the document in my hand. "Is it real?" I asked Mama. "We can truly leave Austria?" I didn't want to let myself hope. Just that day, we'd been spat at twice while we waited in the street to be seen. And on the way home I'd been tripped up by a boy walking the other way, just to make his friends laugh. And they did.

People laughed at us every day now. They called us names whenever they saw us. They delighted in letting us know our place in Nazi-run society.

Not that we needed reminding.

Our place was at the bottom of the heap. Nothing came below the Jews.

"It's real," Mama insisted as she took a chair into her bedroom. "Here, help me reach the cases."

I followed her into her room and held the chair while she climbed up to reach the shelf at the top of her wardrobe. She pulled down two cases. We were allowed one each. One case each to fit our whole lives into. That was it.

By the end of the week, our home would officially belong to the Nazi regime, along with everything in it. All we would own would be whatever we could fit into two cases, and our passports with the big red J for "Jew" stamped on them, in case anyone mistook us for something other than the dregs of society.

I took my case to my bedroom and began to pack. Soon it was almost filled with clothes, books, a few toys, and some odds and ends.

I opened the drawer by my bed and took out the photograph from my ninth birthday.

Sitting on the side of my bed, I squinted at the photo. It was hard to believe it was only three years ago. It felt like a lifetime. The carefree smiles on our faces—I couldn't imagine smiling so freely like that ever again.

The last happy day of my childhood and the day we had met Mr. and Mrs. Stewart. A tickle and a chase and a trip over a lady's foot. And to make up for it, an extra ride on the Ferris wheel and a piece of Sachertorte. That was what we had given them.

And in return they were offering us a whole new life.

Elsa

"Children, hurry. We haven't got long," Mutti whispers.

Vati is already at the door, looking down the street. I pull my rucksack onto my shoulders and pick up the other bag I'm allowed to take. As well as some practical things, I managed to fit in two of my favorite dresses and one pair of shiny shoes. I couldn't bear to leave without them.

I wonder briefly if there's anything else I should have brought. I cannot possibly answer the question as I have no idea how long I will be gone, so I push it away and follow my family out of the house.

In the black of the night, Vati softly closes our door behind us, and the four of us scurry like field mice down the street.

All the way to the station, I dream up scenarios that help take the pain away.

The whole of the last three years has been a dream. I will wake up in a moment and find myself back in Vienna. We never even moved away from there.

Leo and Max will turn up around the next corner, telling me they are coming too. The three of us will go together to the same house in England.

Greta will be waiting at the station.

All the "No Jews" signs around the city will disappear. Nobody really hates us. It was all just a bad, bad, awful nightmare. Someone is waiting at the station to tell us that it is not real, any of it.

None of these things happen.

Vati walks ahead, checking around every corner before we get there, looking all around constantly, signaling for us to follow him. We follow behind him, slightly slower than usual as Otto's limp is playing up a little. That happens when he is stressed or tired. So we pick our way carefully and stealthily through the streets.

And then we are there. We can see the crowds at Prague's main station. Tears are flowing down Mutti's cheeks so fast she doesn't even try to stop them. She grips my hand on one side and Otto's on the other.

"My darlings, my darlings," she says over and over. "I love you so much."

Then don't send us away. The words burn my throat, but I keep them inside.

Vati beckons us toward him. He opens his arms wide, and Otto and I fling ourselves into them.

"We will see you soon," he says fiercely as Mutti joins the hug, wrapping the two of us in a cocoon. "We will never stop thinking about you, not for one day or one hour or even one second."

My tears are soaking his coat. I can feel Mutti's body shaking with sobs.

And then—

"Mr. Bauer, Mr. Bauer!" Someone is calling Vati's name.

We move apart to see a man running toward us. I recognize him as Mr. Janek, one of Vati's friends. He and Vati fought together when Vati joined up to fight Hitler's army last year. He's been to our home. One of the few who still comes. He came only a few weeks ago with his friend Mr. Havel. They were sitting on the sofa together when I came into the kitchen. I think they were holding hands. They broke apart quickly when they saw me. I asked Mutti about them afterward.

"The Nazis don't only hate the Jews," she said bitterly. "They hate anyone who doesn't conform to their ideas of what a 'pure' human being should be like. Even if the reason they hate is for love."

I didn't really understand what she meant, but I knew one thing. Mr. Janek and Mr. Havel were Mutti and Vati's friends, and those were so few and far between nowadays that I had no doubt whatsoever that they were my friends too.

Mr. Janek has reached us now. Up ahead, the crowds at the station seem to be dispersing. What's happening?

"The—train—isn't—going. They won't let it leave," Mr. Janek says. He's panting, and his words come out in staccato bursts.

"Why not?" Vati asks. "Can the children get on the next

one?" Even as he speaks, people are passing us to leave the station. Parents in tears, children running behind them.

While Mr. Janek catches his breath, Vati grabs the arm of a father passing us with his three children. "What's going on? What's happening?"

"Haven't you heard?" the man replies, holding tightly on to the hand of the smallest child, a young girl with a tiny bag on her back.

Vati turns back to Mr. Janek. "Filip, what's happening?" he repeats.

"It's over," Mr. Janek replies. "There are no more trains. The Kindertransport is finished."

"Finished?" Mutti repeats. "Why?"

"Because war has been declared."

At the word "war," I swear I feel the insides of my stomach roll over. I think I'm going to be sick.

"We can no longer run the trains. It is not safe for the children. Go home, all of you," Mr. Janek says.

"And do what?" Mutti asks, her voice high-pitched, almost a squeak.

Mr. Janek shrugs, his arms out wide. "That I cannot tell you," he says. "No one knows what will happen now. But you should hurry, before the authorities come. Go home. Lie low. Wait it out. That is your only option now."

Vati reaches out to shake Mr. Janek's hand. "Thank you for trying," he says. "Thank you for everything."

"I'm sorry I couldn't do better," he replies. "I owe you my life.

Without you fighting beside me last year, I would not be here now. I wanted to repay you. I'm sorry."

Vati puts his arms around Mr. Janek. Mr. Janek reaches out to hug Vati. They stand there together for a moment before pulling away, both wiping tears from their eyes. And that—out of everything—is what breaks me. I've never seen Vati cry. Never. Not once. Not when we left our life in Vienna, nor when he left us to join the army.

The fact that he is crying now makes a poisonous snake of fear wriggle inside me.

Finally Vati pats Mr. Janek on the arm and turns back to us. "Come on," he says, opening his arms to gather us by his side. "Let's go home."

As we walk home in the still-dark night, Mutti tries to be cheerful. "Let's look on the bright side," she says.

"Bright side?" Vati asks.

"We're together! We will stay together, as a family. There will be no goodbyes. My heart will not be broken today."

Vati takes her hand and replies more gently, "That *is* the bright side."

He stops walking and crouches to look me and Otto in the eyes. "Your mother is right," he says. "We are together. We wanted to send you away for safety, but it didn't happen, not tonight. So from this moment on, let's make a promise. We face everything as a family. We are one unit. Your mother and I will be honest with you, we will involve you in all the decisions that affect you. Our country is at war now, and that will change everything."

"Perhaps it means that one day, the Jews will be able to do things like other people can again," Otto says.

Vati reaches out to touch his chin. "I think that is exactly what it means," he says. "The world is not going to let Hitler get away with any more of this nonsense."

"So we keep our heads down, we do what we're told, we don't stand out, and we wait it out," Mutti says.

"Exactly," Vati says. "And before we know it, this will all be over and done with, and we can get on with our lives again. But we will never let anyone separate us. Whatever happens, we face it as a family, together. Agreed?"

The three of us respond in unison. "Agreed."

As we walk home through the streets, my mind races with happy thoughts. I'm not going to be sent away. I don't have to leave my parents. The world is going to make Hitler stop being so horrible.

Any day now I will once again be able to ride my bike, go to the swimming pool, walk in the park! I can hardly believe such things might ever be possible again.

Despite the dark, the cold, the damp streets, I walk home with a smile on my face and a skip in my step.

Everything is going to be all right. I can feel it in my bones and in my heart, and I can't wait to tell Greta.

Leo

When we arrived at the border with Germany, the train stopped and guards came aboard. As they entered our carriage, my mouth was so dry I was finding it hard to breathe, never mind swallow or speak.

Mama handed over our passports and visa documents. The guard opened the passports on the pages with our names, photos, and the big red J that marked us out for special attention.

He nudged the guard next to him. "Jews," he said in a voice filled with so much disgust you would think he was saying "dog poo." I guess to him we were as bad as dog poo.

The other guard took the documents from his colleague and studied them for what felt like an hour before looking up at us and pointing a thumb at the door. "Wrong carriage," he said.

Mama glanced at me, then back at the guard. "Wrong carriage?" she repeated.

"Get out of this carriage," the guard said in a cold voice.

"But—but we have documents," Mama said. "We have tickets for these seats. We are legal."

The guard took a step closer to Mama. So close that, when he replied, spit came out of his mouth and landed on her cheek. "You are Jews. *Nothing* about you is legal."

I tugged at her arm. "Mama, let's just do what he says," I whispered.

With a sigh, Mama reached up for her case. I helped her get it down before grabbing mine and following her to the door. The guards were still checking documents for the other passengers. Each one took just a few seconds, and documents were returned with smiles and nods.

"Where do we go?" Mama asked.

"Last carriage," one of the guards muttered. He didn't even turn around.

"Hurry," said the other one. "Train leaves in two minutes. And we don't wait for Jews."

We scurried off the train and quickly made our way down the platform.

The last carriage had a sign on it. *Dogs, Jews, and Gypsies.*

Mama looked at me. Her cheeks were flushed with shame.

Just then a whistle blew.

"Mama, please, let's get inside. At least we're still on the train," I said.

She pulled a door open, and we glanced inside.

A man and woman were huddled together in a corner on the floor. The woman was wearing a long purple skirt and a loose white shirt, with a yellow scarf wrapped around her head. She was holding a small bundle in her arms. A baby.

The man wore brown trousers and a white shirt with a waistcoat. His face was dark with stubble, and he lifted his black beret and nodded as we opened the door. I clambered aboard. The man was on his feet and beside me in seconds.

"Let me help," he said, reaching out to take Mama's bags and help her aboard.

A second later, the door slammed behind us and we were in total darkness.

"Here, follow me," the man said, and we felt our way along the walls to sit beside him and his wife.

As my eyes adjusted to the darkness, I could see that along one side of the carriage were rows of crates. Most were empty. The one nearest to us had a Labrador inside it who whined like a crying child. There were no seats anywhere.

"You are Jewish?" the woman asked as she spread her blanket for Mama to sit beside her on the floor.

Mama's face tightened as she readied herself for the attack that usually followed us being identified as Jews. "Why?" she asked.

The woman put a hand on Mama's arm. "We are your friends,"

she said softly. "We are Roma. The ones the Nazis call 'Gypsies.'" She gestured around us at the cages and the bare, cold carriage. "We are told our place, just like you. I am Kizzy, and this is my husband, Mairik."

Mama talked quietly with Kizzy and Mairik as the train chugged along. They were heading to Holland, like us. They were planning to join friends in the Roma community who had managed to sponsor them for visas.

As I sat in the darkness, my thoughts flashed to Elsa. Where was she now? Our contact had been less and less frequent, and I hadn't heard from her at all since Hitler had moved into Czechoslovakia. Every day I woke with worries in my mind, carried them around with me all day, and took them to bed with me at night—and Elsa was always high on my list, beside Papa. I just hoped things weren't as bad in Prague as they were in Vienna.

Max still came into my thoughts too, but I didn't worry so much about him. I hadn't heard from him at all since he'd left for Munich, even though I had written to him many times. He'd managed to slip me his new address before they left. I guessed he was too busy to reply. I hoped that was the reason. I refused to torture myself by imagining other possibilities. Besides, he wasn't Jewish, so I hoped that meant he was safe, although who knew anymore.

I tried to make myself comfortable on the floor. I was next to the cage with the dog in it. I named him Benji. Through the holes in his basket, I stroked his golden hair. He stopped crying and snuffled his nose into my hand, wagging his tail softly against the side of the cage.

Finally the train came to a standstill and we could hear doors being opened. Our carriage didn't have a window, so we couldn't be sure what was going on. But the train had been still for a while and we could hear voices on the platform.

We got up and dusted ourselves down. "Thank you for sharing the journey," Mama said to our new friends. She and Kizzy hugged while Mairik reached out to shake my hand.

"Good luck," he said.

Next thing we knew, the door was flung open. The daylight was blinding and I covered my eyes.

A guard reached in and grabbed my arm. "Come," he said.

Mama and I followed him out of the carriage and along the platform to a building where others were lining up. We joined them in the line. It happened too quickly for me to see what the guards had done with Kizzy and Mairik and their baby.

"Excuse me," Mama said to a couple in front of us. "Where are we, please?"

The couple turned around. I recognized them from the carriage we'd been dragged out of at the start of the journey. The woman sniffed and made a face at us before very deliberately reaching into her pocket for a tissue, which she then used to cover her nose.

The man said, "Customs," before putting an arm around his wife as they both turned away.

"We're just Jewish," I mumbled under my breath. "Don't worry, you can't catch it."

Up ahead, it seemed that everyone just had to show their passports and documents and was then instructed to head left, over to a train that was waiting on the next platform.

"This is it, the border," Mama said. The first major step in our journey to England. We were only a few feet away from being out of Germany. Despite the way we had traveled to get there and the response of the people around us, Mama couldn't keep the excitement out of her voice.

The line moved quickly, and soon we were at the front. Mama handed over our documents, and we waited while the guard peered at them, reading every word of the signed letter from the Stewarts, checking every inch of our visas, looking us up and down as though we were filth.

And then he nodded at a cubicle to our right. "That way," he said.

Everyone else had been sent to the left, where a door took them straight onto the opposite platform. The one with the waiting train on it. I glanced around to see where Kizzy and Mairik had gone with the baby. I couldn't see them.

Please let them arrive safely.

"We are going to England," Mama said. "We have a boat from Holland. We have to catch that train."

The guard looked at her as he might look at an animal that

had just spoken back to him. I didn't need reminding that, to him, that was exactly what *had* just happened.

He pointed again at the cubicle. "In there," he growled.

We had no choice. By now, almost oblivious to the stares and the sneers as we'd had so many of them, we left the line of people and went over to the cubicle. Leaving our cases on the floor, we sat on a bench and waited.

Another guard came in after a few minutes. Like all the others, he wore a brown uniform, with a gun in a holster on his polished leather belt. "Get up," he said. "No sitting allowed." Then he pointed at our cases. "Put them on the bench and open them."

We weren't even allowed to sit down now? I lugged my case onto the bench and stood beside it. Mama did the same. Even our bags had more rights than us.

The guard pulled out everything, turning clothes inside out, throwing papers around, dropping objects on the floor. When he came to a small, old blanket, I felt Mama stiffen beside me. Why did she care so much about a moth-eaten blanket?

Then I remembered. It was the one she had sewn her wedding ring into. I closed my little finger around hers. The guard tossed the blanket aside with the rest of her belongings and moved on to my case.

Again, he manhandled every possession I had. I held my breath as I watched him, with only one thought in my mind.

Do what you like with my clothes, but please don't take away my precious photograph.

Soon he was done. The photo was still safely in the pages of a book.

We folded our belongings away as quickly as we could and closed our cases. I started to relax. It hadn't been too bad.

Then he spoke again. "Get undressed."

Mama just stared at him. With one hand, he pulled aside a curtain in the middle of the room. With the other, he pulled his jacket aside to remind us of the gun in its holster. "In there," he said to her. Mama didn't try to argue this time. She walked across to the other section of the cubicle.

"And you," he said to me as he drew the curtain closed behind her.

I undressed as quickly as I could. The guard took my clothes and examined them as I stood there shivering. I kept asking myself what was making me shiver more: the cold or my fear. It was a tough contest.

"Turn around," the guard said. I did as I was told. Finally he threw my clothes back at me. "Get dressed," he barked as he went behind the curtain to humiliate Mama in the same way.

Finally we were allowed to leave the cubicle.

"Where do we go now?" Mama asked, pulling her coat back on and picking up her case.

"You go to hell as far as I'm concerned," the guard said before turning away.

We took that as our cue to follow the rest of the passengers to the other platform.

163

"Mama, come quickly," I urged. A man was walking up the platform, blowing a whistle and closing doors.

We ran across to the train and got to the last open door a second before the guard did. I threw our cases onto the train, jumped aboard, and reached down to help Mama get on behind me.

And then the door closed, the whistle blew, the train started moving, and we were off.

Mama and I looked at each other and grinned. Then, despite the ordeal we'd just been through, we threw our arms around each other in joy; we jumped and danced and sang and laughed.

I wished more than anything that Papa were there to share the moment with us.

I did what you told me, Papa, I said to him in my mind. *I got Mama to safety.*

And then I smiled and smiled and smiled. We really had done it. We had crossed the border. We were no longer in Germany. The Nazis would never again rule our lives.

1940

Max

ax spent even longer than usual in his bedroom shining his boots, combing his hair, and checking the creases in his shorts. It was a special day, and he knew how important it was to get everything right.

"Ready?" His father was at the door.

"Nearly, Father."

"Hurry. We leave in five minutes sharp. I don't want to have to explain to my driver that my son has kept him waiting."

"You won't have to, Father. I promise," Max assured him. His father gave a quick nod before leaving Max and closing the door behind him.

Max glanced in the mirror one last time to check that his hair was parted perfectly, his Hitler Youth shirt was buttoned up correctly, his neckerchief was straight. He slid the swastika arm-band onto his sleeve and stood to attention. Thrusting his right arm forward, he uttered, *"Heil Hitler!"* to his reflection.

Yes. He was ready.

The drive took a little under an hour. Max had not been this far out of Munich since they'd moved there. And he had never been to his father's place of work. He'd told his friends what he was doing today, and they were all envious.

"It's so unfair," his friend Hans had complained. "Why do you get such an important father?"

Max had shrugged. "I guess I'm just lucky," he'd said.

And he certainly felt it. Just last week, at another Hitler Youth weekend camp, he had been praised for his crisp marching style, led his team to victory in the relay races, *and* been awarded a new badge for his uniform, for his survival skills. He was popular, too. He no longer even remembered the days when he could count his friends on the fingers of one hand. And now he was going to get firsthand experience of the Nazi regime at work alongside his father.

"Lucky" was the word!

The car came to a stop outside some big gates. They were heav-ily locked, with soldiers parading along both sides, rifles over their shoulders and eyes darting around everywhere like eagles'. Above a door in the center of the gates, the iron had three words wrought into it: *Arbeit Macht Frei*. Work sets you free.

Max's chest filled with pride. He could hardly believe that he was really here. That he was allowed to be a part of this.

"Here we are," his father said as he got out of the car, indicating for Max to follow him.

The soldiers at the gates snapped their heels together when they saw Max's father. *"Heil Hitler!"* they shouted. Max's father returned the salute. Max stood beside him and thrust his arm forward. *"Heil Hitler!"* he said along with his father.

One of the soldiers laughed as he unlocked the gate. "I see we have a new guard today," he said, pointing at Max.

Max's father appraised his son before replying lightly, "Perhaps one day. When he is a man."

Max puffed his chest out. Why could his father not see that he *was* a man? He was twelve years old, for goodness' sake. He wasn't a child! Everyone else could see it. Why did his father still treat him like a little kid?

Max decided to take a risk. "I hope so, sir," he replied, kicking his heels together and standing to attention.

The soldier laughed again. "Look at you," he said. "You'll be one of us before long. I'll look out for you." He pulled the gate open to let them come through. "Welcome to Dachau."

As Max followed his father through the gate, he felt as if the words above the door held a magical power just for him. He had never felt so light, so capable of anything.

They walked along a concrete path. Long white buildings with tiny windows lined the path on both sides.

"I have some paperwork to do first of all," his father said as he opened a door into one of the buildings and they entered a small office. He pointed at a chair in the corner of the room. "Sit there, keep quiet and wait, and then I'll show you around."

Max did what he was told. He watched as various soldiers came into the room with forms for his father to check and sign. He listened as his father barked orders to men who instantly jumped to fulfill them.

"Yes, sir. *Heil Hitler!*" they would say, standing to attention and saluting before they left the room.

Max already knew that his father was an important man, but being with him at work made Max realize that he had never understood quite *how* important the man was. He was one of the top officers of this whole place!

Watching him work—his efficiency, his clarity, the respect he had from all of his staff—Max swore to himself that he would be just like him one day.

"Right." The paperwork was finished, and his father checked his watch as he got up from his seat. "Midday. You want to see how we do roll call around here?"

"Yes, please!" Max jumped up and followed his father out of the office. They walked along the concrete path between the buildings.

To their right, from behind the buildings and stretching ahead, high poles stood at regular intervals. They were joined together with rows and rows of barbed wire and ran as far ahead as Max could see.

"Don't go near those," his father instructed when he saw Max looking. "They are electric. It'll kill you if you touch them."

Max could see soldiers parading the length of the fence. He hoped none of them accidentally tripped and got electrified.

His father was still walking, and Max ran to catch up. They turned into a big square in the center of the camp. Ahead of them Max could see rows and rows of low buildings.

"That's the barracks where the workers live," his father said.

"Workers?" Max asked. "You mean the soldiers?"

His father's mouth did the nearest thing it got to a smile. Then he shook his head. "The soldiers are loyal Nazis," he said. "No. I mean the prisoners. The ones who have no use to society. The Jews, the Poles, the Gypsies, the homosexuals, the criminals. We protect everyone else by containing them here and putting them to good use. You could say we are doing a service to the German people by keeping these vermin off their streets."

"I see," Max said. He'd learned to keep his face completely passive when his father or anyone else said things like this—even if it still made a tiny part of him twitch inside. The twitchy bit got smaller and smaller every time, and got buried deeper and deeper— so deep, in fact, that sometimes he didn't even notice what was being said or register anything wrong with it.

The days when he'd agonized over whether such words applied to his old friends were long gone. It was easier just to ignore it and not think about it too much.

"Here they come now," his father said.

Max watched as a huge group of men came toward them, marching in between the barracks to the square. On each side of the group, SS soldiers watched the men as they marched beside them. Most of the soldiers had their rifles by their sides, while a couple of them pointed the weapons toward the prisoners in the middle. The soldiers looked so smart in their uniforms, and Max found himself standing straighter as the men marched toward him and his father. He hoped they could see how much effort he had made with his uniform.

The prisoners were a different matter entirely. There were lots of them: hundreds, maybe even more, Max thought. They didn't march with the sharp snap of boots and the high kicks of their legs like the soldiers. And their uniforms were shabby and dirty. They didn't even seem to be trying to look smart. Max couldn't help agreeing with his father. Real Germans were better off with these people kept away from them.

As Max watched, the men were marched toward them and told to halt right in front of him and his father.

Max's father glared at them in silence for a few moments. Then, with no warning, he suddenly bellowed, "Numbers. Now!"

Instantly the prisoners started calling out numbers, one at a time. If any of them didn't shout loud enough or paused too long before shouting a number, the nearest guard would nudge them in the side with his rifle.

Max even saw one man get punched in the stomach so hard he fell to the ground. Max let out a small gasp before he could stop himself, and glanced up instinctively to make sure his father hadn't heard him. He didn't need to worry. His father was staring intently at the group, his eyes popping like they were on fire, his neck taut, a line of sweat dotting his forehead.

The roll call seemed to go on forever. Eventually his father nodded at one of the soldiers. "Take over," he said. "Lunch. But not too much. We don't want them getting fat now, do we?" He laughed as he said that, and the soldier did too. Max didn't really get the joke but laughed along to show that he knew his father was funny and clever.

"Come," his father said. "We'll get *our* lunch too." He started to walk toward the main building.

Max saw that his bootlace had come loose and quickly bent down to tie it before his father noticed. The prisoners had started to disperse, each coming past him to collect a small tin bowl of something that looked like cold porridge.

As Max stood up, one of the prisoners caught his eye.

"Max?" he said.

Max's insides turned cold. Why was this filthy, scruffy prisoner saying his name? He looked at the man more closely. His face was gaunt and gray, covered in scabs and scratches and grime. His outfit was a misshapen gray suit—it looked more like pajamas than a uniform. His dirty hands held an equally dirty bowl. Max thought he had never looked at anyone so disgusting.

And yet, there was something familiar about him.

Then the man did something Max hadn't seen anyone do since he'd entered Dachau. He smiled. His teeth were black and rotten. Those he had, anyway. At least half of them were missing.

"Max, it's me," the man said. "Mr. Grunberg."

Mr. Grunberg? The name rolled toward Max like a rock gathering speed as it hurtled down a hill. Leo's father!

No. It couldn't be. There was a mistake. Leo's father was always the best-dressed man in town. He was twice as wide as this man— and had twice as many teeth. He always looked immaculate. He wouldn't be caught dead walking around like this in an ill-fitting uniform with buttons missing and covered in mud. He wasn't even wearing shoes!

And why would he be here? With these prisoners? The man who used to make everyone laugh? It couldn't be him. It couldn't.

But the smile. Even with half his teeth missing and the other half rotting, it was definitely familiar. His eyes. Among the grayness of everything about him—and everything about Dachau, come to think of it—they still twinkled in a way that danced like light on a speck of dust.

"You remember me, don't you?" Mr. Grunberg was saying.

Just then, Max's father turned back to him. "Max! Come!" he bellowed before continuing to march ahead.

Without thinking about it, Max did something that came so instinctively he didn't even have time to be ashamed of himself. Just like he had done that other time, when his best friend was humiliated in assembly.

He moved away from the scruffy, dirty man. "I don't know you," he said, shaking his head. "You've got the wrong person."

And then he ran as fast as he could to follow his father to the

174

warmth and comfort of the officers' dining room and join him for a hearty three-course lunch. As he ate, he banished any thoughts of Leo, Leo's father, his old school—his old life—from his mind. Those thoughts had no place in his world. He shut them out with an imaginary gate as big, as hard, and as cold as the one at the entrance to Dachau.

Elsa

I'm in bed, fast asleep, when I hear noises downstairs.

I sit up and rub my eyes. Doors slamming. Raised voices. Something that sounds like furniture being thrown around.

Are Mutti and Vati having an argument?

The idea is ridiculous. I have never in my life heard my parents argue. At the absolute most, they have maybe disagreed over minor decisions in quiet voices. They would never argue like this.

Otto appears at my door. His face is white.

"What's going on?" I ask him as I push the covers off and get out of bed.

"Soldiers," he says simply.

"In our *home?*"

He nods, then puts a finger over his lips, and together we creep out of my bedroom and across the landing to the top of the stairs, where we can listen without being seen.

"You can't just go around trashing my home like this!" Vati is shouting at someone.

A voice I don't recognize—I guess one of the soldiers—replies, "That's what I am telling you. This is no longer your home."

I look at Otto. "Not our home?" I whisper. What does that mean? Of course it's our home.

"I'm going downstairs. I need to know what's going on. Come on," Otto says.

But I'm nowhere near as brave as Otto, and the last thing I want to do is talk to the soldiers who have said this is not our home anymore. Or maybe that's the *second*-to-last thing I want to do. The last thing I want is to be left on my own. So I meekly follow Otto down the stairs, doing my best to hide behind him as he strides into the kitchen.

"Mutti, Vati, what's going on?" Otto asks.

Mutti rushes toward us. "Go back upstairs, darling," she urges. "Nothing's going on."

But Vati holds an arm out to stop her. "They need to know, Stella," he says. "There's no point in pretending it's not happening."

One of the soldiers wags a finger at Vati. "See," he says, turning to the other two soldiers and laughing. "At least one of these stupid Jews has finally understood what's going on."

"Vati?" I ask.

He crouches down and talks quietly. "We have to leave," he says.

"Leave where?" I ask. "Our home? Prague? Czechoslovakia?"

"Just our home," Vati says.

"For now," one of the soldiers says with a laugh, and the three of them guffaw.

I can see Otto's jaw tightening and his hand curling into a fist. I reach out for his hand.

"We have to live somewhere else for a while," Mutti says, coming over to join us. She takes my other hand. "We'll all be together, like we promised. We just have to move to a different house."

"Why can't we stay in this one?" I ask. My voice comes out in much more of a whine than I want it to. "This is our home."

"Not any longer, it isn't," one of the soldiers replies. "You Jews don't get to own a home anymore. It's your own fault for choosing to live somewhere so nice. Much too nice for a family of Jews. And so near to our headquarters, too. Perfect for us."

"You can't just take our home from us," Otto says to the soldiers.

One of them steps toward us. I flinch and take a tiny step back. "Actually, we can," he sneers, his face right in front of Otto's. "We can do whatever we want." Then he moves to me. "We don't like Jews. And we need your house. So you're moving. Understand?"

I nod fiercely.

He glances at his friends, and they both grin back at him. One of them jumps up to sit on the table—the kitchen table where we've eaten our dinner every evening for the last three years. He pulls a chair around, and as he puts his feet on it, he reaches for the silver candlesticks that we have had for as long as I can remember.

We barely used them when I was younger. Neither of my parents had ever been religious, and we didn't practice the traditions or rituals of our faith. That's changed a little since coming to Prague. Only a little. Vati takes us to shul on Saturday mornings when he can, and every Friday night Mutti lights candles in these candlesticks and says a *brachah*—a blessing—over them. I like it: the feeling of being part of something bigger than myself.

And now the soldier is waving the candlesticks at his friend as if they mean nothing at all. "What d'you think of these? They'd make a nice present for Helga, eh?"

One of the others makes a vulgar move with his body and replies, "Oh yes, she'll be *very* grateful for a present like that!"

The soldier sitting on the table laughs as he reaches down to put them in his bag.

Vati is in front of him, his hands clasped together as if in a prayer. "I beg you," he says. "Please do not take them. They have been in my wife's family for three generations."

The soldier looks him in the eye and replies lightly, "Well, they're not in your family any longer."

"Please, let us keep this one thing. They are so special to us," Vati insists.

"That is a good lesson to learn," the soldier says softly, and for a moment I think he has understood how important they are and

179

will let us keep them. Then, in a snarling voice, he adds, "Now you will understand that you Jews own nothing!"

He jumps down from the table and shoves the candlesticks into his bag. "You've got twenty-four hours to pack," he says. "We'll be back to move in tomorrow."

Tomorrow? I am to pack the contents of my life overnight? What should I take this time? The last time I packed a case, I still thought fine dresses and shiny shoes were important and had packed them carefully with my other belongings. Something tells me I will have less reason to wear jolly clothes where we're going.

Beckoning to the others to join him, the soldier crosses the kitchen. "One day," he repeats at the door. "We will be back for you tomorrow."

When the soldiers have left, I head up to my bedroom to start the process of packing up my life once again. One thought comforts me amid the horror.

After what has just happened, this house no longer feels like home. At least it won't be quite so hard to leave it now.

Leo

I stood in front of my mirror and practiced my smile until it looked convincing. Every morning I did the same thing before leaving for school. Mama had given up so much for us to have this opportunity, and the Stewarts had been so incredibly generous.

The last thing any of them needed was to know how miserable I was at school.

Mama was in the kitchen with Mrs. Stewart. They were sitting together at the table with cookbooks spread out in front of them. I had never known Mama to have a best friend before, but since we'd been in England, she and Mrs. Stewart had been inseparable. Mrs. Stewart had spent hours and hours with her, teaching her English, introducing her to people, helping her adjust to our new life.

The Stewarts had done at least as much for me. They'd found me a place at the local school. They'd converted Mr. Stewart's study into a bedroom for me. They'd even paid to have an English teacher visit twice a week to give me extra lessons.

I could speak pretty good English now. I just couldn't get rid of my accent. That was the issue. Well, it was one of them. That and the fact that I still felt scared every time we left the house. I still flinched when anyone came to the door. I still expected to be told to stand up and move to the back of the room every single morning in assembly.

It was like walking around in a minefield, or being in a permanent nightmare. Sometimes I wondered if Mama felt the same way. I couldn't ask her, though. I couldn't run the risk of upsetting her by letting her know how hard I was finding things.

Every now and then, I would leave my worries behind. Remind myself we were in England now. We were safe. Those moments were like gasping for air after being held underwater. But something would always happen to dunk me back into my nightmare again.

And being teased by the other boys at school didn't help.

"See you later," I said from the doorway, my practiced smile bright on my face.

Mama got up from the table and came to kiss me on the cheek. "Have a lovely day, darling."

"I will, of course. I always do!" I said in my rehearsed cheerful manner.

"You're such a good boy. I'm so glad you're happy here," she said.

I smiled again. I didn't reply this time. I couldn't force any more lies out of my mouth.

Mama waved me off at the door as she did each morning, and I waved back and walked up the road to wait for the bus.

The trouble began at the bus stop, as usual.

"Hey, look, it's the Kraut," said Tim, one of the boys in my year. He was taller than the rest of us and had white-blond hair and blue eyes. He was one of the most popular boys in my year, which meant everyone copied what he did.

Tim had had it in for me from the moment I'd arrived. At first I couldn't understand most of what he said, but the downside of picking up English so quickly was that I soon came to realize he insulted me every time he saw me.

"How are you today, Jerry?" one of Tim's sidekicks, Robert, asked.

"I'm not called Jerry," I mumbled to the ground as I sidled up to the bus stop.

Tim thrust his arm out in a Nazi salute. "*Sieg heil!* I am NOT called Jerry. Zat is NOT my name," he said in an exaggerated German accent. The other boys laughed. "And if you call me zat, zen I vill shoot you!"

More laughter.

I felt bile rise in my throat. *Don't you know how wrong you are?* I wanted to scream at them. *Do you not realize your enemy is my enemy too?*

Anything I said would only encourage them, so I kept quiet and fiddled with the hem of my school jacket as I stared at the pavement.

"Come on, Jerry, we're only kidding," a boy called Daniel said, nudging my arm.

"I'm *not* called Jerry," I said again.

"But you're German. You're the enemy. That's what we call *all* the Germans," Daniel said. "It's just a nickname. It's not personal."

Luckily, the bus came along then and the boys all dispersed to separate seats as we got on board. Respite. For now.

I shuffled down the aisle, alone with my thoughts.

Back in Vienna, everyone hated us because we were Jewish. Here they hated me because of my accent. Would there ever be a place where I could simply fit in and be accepted for who I was? What would these boys say if I told them the truth? *I'm not German, I'm Jewish, so hate me for that instead.*

I doubted it would help.

There was only one seat left on the bus. It was next to Daniel. Out of them all, he was the least awful.

"You shouldn't take it to heart so much," he said as the bus started up. He spoke quietly, so no one else would hear. "The more they see they've upset you, the more they'll do it. Act like you don't care. Laugh with them. Tease them back. Show that you're one of us, and you'll be accepted before you know it."

"But I'm *not* one of you," I said.

"Okay, you've got a bit of an accent," he agreed. "But so what?"

I shook my head. "It's not that." I lowered my voice even further.

Finally I couldn't hold it back any longer. "I'm Jewish," I said.

Daniel stared at me. Now I'd done it. I'd blown it with the one boy who didn't bully me relentlessly every day. A wave of fear engulfed me. What if Daniel was a Nazi? What if they all were? What if it was all going to happen here as well, just like in Vienna, just like in Czechoslovakia and Germany? Hitler could march into England any day, and that would be it. Game over.

My palms were hot and slippy with sweat, and I was about to tell Daniel I was joking when he leaned in further. "So am I," he said.

My jaw fell so wide open it almost hurt. "What?" I hissed. "You're Jewish?"

"There isn't a synagogue in this town and we've never been part of a bigger community—but yeah, we light candles on Friday nights and we don't eat bread at Passover." Daniel shrugged. "I'm Jewish. What's the big deal?"

"But—but you're just like all the others! They don't tease you, they don't bully you. You're one of the gang!"

Daniel pulled a face. "Why shouldn't I be one of the gang?" he asked. "It's not a crime to be Jewish, you know."

I actually laughed at that point. He had literally no idea. No idea that, actually, it really had been a crime to be Jewish in my old life.

But maybe it was me who had no idea. No real belief that those days were over and we really were safe in England. Daniel was right. I hadn't done anything wrong, and I had to stop acting as though I had.

I had to start living again.

It was time to start telling myself I was safe. We'd escaped. We had nothing to fear in Britain.

So I smiled at Daniel. "No, you're right," I said. "It's not a crime at all. I'm only kidding."

"See, that's more like it," he said. "Just keep smiling like that. If someone says something stupid to you, don't let them know it's bothered you. Brush it off. Tease them back. You'll fit in with us in no time."

By the time we got to school and Daniel and I sat next to each other for attendance and nudged each other in assembly and sent notes to each other in class, I realized I had something I hadn't had for years. Something I hadn't had since Max and Elsa had left Vienna.

I had a friend.

1941

Elsa

Where we live now isn't too bad. We were moved to a tenement block on the poor side of town. We were among
the first to be moved here. Like the Nazi soldiers said, it
was our misfortune to have been in a house so near to their headquarters that we were evicted so early on.

The rest of Prague's Jews weren't that far behind us. All of this
year, Jewish families have been having their homes taken from
them and sent to live in these tenement blocks. Being so close to
so many Jewish people is almost fun, in a strange sort of way. It's
like we're one big family, a community of people all in it together.
The best things about it are:

1. My family are close to me all the time.

2. Greta is here too. She and her parents came a few months after we did, so we can still see each other as much as we want. They live in the same block, a couple of floors below us.

3. Greta and I have adopted a cat. We have called him Felix, and he is the sweetest little creature you have ever seen. He is always outside our block waiting for us whenever we go out, and he meows and arches his back really high when we stroke him. He is mostly black but has little white paws that look like socks and a tiny white spot on his nose. After my family and Greta and the boys, who I still love even though I never see them, Felix is my favorite thing ever in the world.

The worst things about living here are:

1. It is very crowded. I don't know how many there are of us now in this block, but we share our three-bedroom apartment with three other families. That's one family in each bedroom and the fourth in the lounge. With one bathroom between us.

2. The rats. (Although, we sometimes let Felix into the apartment, as he helps chase these away.)

3. There's nowhere to wash our clothes, so everything is quite dirty.

4. We are hungry a lot, as Jews are not allowed to work, so
   we have very little money to buy food. And yes, Greta
   and I make that worse for ourselves by sharing what little
   we get with Felix. But we have agreed that it is worth it
   for the cuddles and purrs we get in thanks.

Even with all those things, every morning when I wake up, I remind myself that I'm lucky. I have somewhere to live. It might be crowded, but at least it is warm and dry. Mostly. It wasn't too bad in the summer, but now that the autumn nights have started to draw in, the cold is seeping through the walls—and so is the rain.

But at least we have a roof over our heads. And we are still here and still together.

Mutti and Vati are glad that I have a friend. Greta and I meet in each other's apartments every chance we get. We talk about anything and everything, like we always have done.

I sometimes can't believe I have only known her a couple of years. I feel like I've known her all my life. We are almost like sisters.

"What do you want to be when we grow up?" Greta asks me today as we sit together on the wall outside the tenement building, feeding tiny morsels of bread to Felix. It's one of our favorite questions.

"Alive?" I reply.

Greta laughs and nudges me in the side. "No. Really. What would you be if you could be anything?"

I think for a moment. "I'm embarrassed to say it," I say eventually.

Greta leans in closer. "Go on. I won't tell anyone."

I shrug. "I think I'd just like to be a wife. I want to get married and have three children and stay at home and cook beautiful meals."

Greta laughs. "Who will you marry?" she asks me. "Let me guess . . ."

I laugh too. "Maybe Max or Leo," I say. "Unless someone else asks me first."

The truth is, I can barely picture Max and Leo anymore. I still have the photograph of the three of us, packed tightly in a case with my clothes, but I rarely look at it nowadays, and without it I can hardly even conjure up their faces in my mind.

I still think about them. I wonder if they've moved as many times as I have. I wonder if Leo is still safe in Vienna, if Max is happy in Munich, if they ever think about me.

I wonder if I will ever see either of them again.

And then my heart hurts and I have to change the subject. "What about you?" I ask Greta. "What will you be?"

Greta talks in a whisper. "I'm going to be a resistance fighter," she says.

"What's that?" I ask.

"I've heard of young women who are joining the fight against Hitler. They run secret errands, and no one suspects them because they're only girls. What d'you think?"

What I think is that the thought terrifies me. I couldn't bear for Greta to go off and do something so dangerous. I cannot lose the only friend I've got.

"I think you're the bravest person I've ever known," I say.

Greta hugs me, then feeds Felix the last few crumbs and picks him up for a cuddle. "And when we've won the war and sent Hitler packing, I shall marry one of your boys," she says. "And we will live in a big house in the country and have seven cats."

I laugh as I watch her playing with Felix. These moments with Greta are everything. Her friendship makes me feel alive.

And that's about as good a feeling as any of us have around here nowadays, so I know it's something to treasure.

Leo

It was Saturday morning and I was awake early because I was meeting my friends at the park. I was scrabbling under my bed looking for my shoes when I heard Mama scream from downstairs.

"Leo!" she yelled. "Come quickly!"

Old habits still hadn't left me. My heart thumped so hard I could feel it in my throat. And my mind went to the places it always went to.

It was all over. Everything in England had been a dream, and reality had now caught up with us. The Nazis had found us, and Mama and I were about to be dragged out of a life we had no right to live.

I ran downstairs. Mama was standing in the hall, one hand clapped over her mouth, the other clutching a piece of paper.

"What is it, Mama?" I asked breathlessly. "What's happened? Are you all right?"

She nodded and held out the piece of paper. It was an envelope. She took her hand away from her mouth. As she did, I could see that she was smiling. "It's from your father," she said.

A letter. From Papa. Not the Nazis. Not something bad. Something wonderful.

As I took the envelope from her, my heart kept racing—but with excitement, not fear. The letter was covered in postmarks and scribbles. Our old address in Vienna was crossed out with thick red lines; postmarks declaring numerous posting points and dates covered the whole envelope, and at the top were two stamps. One bore the Nazi eagle picture, and the other was a picture of Adolf Hitler.

Even with all that, I could still recognize the writing beneath the scrawls and stamps and forwarding marks. I would know it anywhere.

"It *is* from Papa!" I cried. I followed the trail of postmarks with my finger. One after another after another until I read the one covering the stamps and discovered something that shocked me. The original date was 1940. Papa's letter had taken a whole year to reach us!

"Come in the kitchen and let's sit by the fire," Mama said. "We can read it in the warmth."

I followed Mama into the kitchen. The room was still in darkness from last night's air raid. We'd had the curtains closed for a blackout for almost twenty-four hours. The raids happened fairly regularly nowadays.

I pulled aside the curtain in the kitchen and opened the envelope as Mama stoked the fire. Then we pulled two stools together and read Papa's letter.

My darling wife and my dearest son,
I hope this letter reaches you. I just want you to know that everything is fine with me. I have been moved to a place called Dachau, where I am working hard alongside many friends and comrades. We are treated well. We sing as we work. We are well fed and well dressed and everything is really great.

And, Leo, guess what? I met your old friend Max the other day! He asked how you were and asked me to send you his fondest regards.

And of course so much of the same from me to you both. I will see you soon, I promise.
My love, always,
Papa

I gripped the letter and stared at the words, reading them over and over. And then a tear fell onto Papa's words and smudged them.

Mama gently covered my hand with hers. "Hey, careful," she said. "This is all we have of him."

She was right. Not only that, but as I read the letter again, I couldn't see any hidden code telling me to disregard his words. That meant they must be true. Papa was safe and well.

I passed the letter back to Mama. The thought of Papa so far away from us, working so hard, sending us a letter that took a year to get to us, hurt so deeply it felt like a football being kicked into the pit of my stomach.

But his words eased the pain. He was fine. He was being fed. He was singing and working and he had friends. And he'd seen Max! My old best friend had sent a message to me across all the miles and all the years. He still thought about me.

After all this time, all the letters I had sent Max without receiving a reply, I had begun to think I would never hear anything of him again. Maybe I had gotten his address wrong. Maybe he had tried to write to me too. It wouldn't have been easy for him. I wasn't a fool. I wasn't a hopeful kid any longer. I knew his father wouldn't want him to write to me.

But he could have found a way. Maybe he had written and his letters had gone astray—and now we were in England and he would have no idea how to find me.

Whatever it was, it didn't matter. He still cared—and he'd seen Papa!

Maybe if I wrote to him again, I could give him my new address and I'd hear back from him. It was worth one more shot.

I'd do it after football. And I could tell him all about my new friends as well! Maybe he'd even meet them one day. I was sure he'd like them, especially Daniel, who was the nearest thing I had to a best friend nowadays.

I looked at the clock on the kitchen wall. "Mama, I have to go. The others will be waiting for me."

Mama was smiling. My heart stopped for a second; I hadn't seen that smile for so long. The warmth of it, the love behind her eyes. It was as if the knowledge that Papa was fine had brought her back from behind a veil where she'd been hiding all this time.

"You go and play," she said, patting my knee. She held Papa's letter against her heart. "I will be here with your father."

I stood up and bent to kiss her forehead. "I love you, Mama," I said.

"I love you too, my wonderful boy," she replied. "Have fun with your friends."

"I will," I said. And I knew it was true.

The feeling Papa's letter had planted inside me kept me warm all day. It made me kick the ball harder, pass it better. It meant I ran around the field with my hands in the air, whooping at the top of my voice when I scored a goal.

It even meant that afterward, when we finished with football and were playing soldiers instead, I didn't mind being the German this time—even when I got shot in the middle of a "*Heil Hitler!*" salute.

It was only a game, after all. We were just having fun. I was with my friends. It was a good day.

Elsa

It's a Saturday morning in late November when they come for us.

We know them quite well by now. The *Judenrat*. The Jewish Council. They visit us at least every month, checking we are all okay, we have enough food to survive, and so on. The Nazis chose them to do their dirty work—and, like us, the *Judenrat* were powerless to say no. In their way, they are no luckier than we are. Especially on days like today when they have come to give us bad news.

They know as well as we do that they could so easily be the next ones to receive such news. They know as well as we do how dispensable they are to the Nazis. They know as well as we do that sending them to do this work on a Saturday—a religious day for Jewish people—is the Nazis' way of making them the butt of their fun as much as it's about reminding us how few rights we have now.

Greta is in our apartment, and we are sitting together, brushing each other's hair with a tiny brush that her mother brought with them when they moved here.

"Your hair is so beautiful," Greta says as she carefully brushes through the matted, knotted mess: the result of never having any shampoo to wash it.

I laugh. "Beautiful? This knotty mop?"

She tugs at a knot. "Your beautiful red hair is the only thing in this whole tenement block that isn't gray!" she insists.

"That and the dreaded stars," I say. Since September, all Jews have had to wear a yellow star on their clothes. I wear it, but I hate it.

Greta shudders. "Let's not think about them," she says quickly. "Let's think about your hair instead. It's my favorite thing."

"My hair is your favorite thing?" I laugh.

Greta stops brushing and comes round to stand in front of me. "Actually, no. *You* are my favorite thing, Elsa," she says. Her eyes burn darkly into me. "Alongside my parents, you are the best thing in my life. You know that, don't you?"

I smile at my best friend. "I know it because I feel the same way," I reply. It's true. I've never had a friend like her. Leo and Max were the best friends I could ever have wanted back in Vienna. But they're not here, they're not sharing this life, these squashed homes, these badges of humiliation on their clothes. And those things are part of the glue that joins me to Greta. She is like my twin, and I honestly can't imagine life without her.

Just as I am about to tell her this, she holds up a finger and says, "Aside from Felix, of course. He comes first."

I can't help smiling. Trust Greta to make me laugh when I'm about to get all sentimental on her. It's one of her top skills. "Of course!" I reply with mock seriousness. "No one can beat Felix!"

Just then, a rap on the front door jolts us both. Mutti and Vati are in the kitchen with one of the other families. Otto is in the lounge with one of the boys.

Vati calls us all together. "Come," he says. "They need to speak to us all."

The man from the Jewish Council waits while all four families squeeze into the lounge.

Once we're all gathered, he clears his throat and looks at the floor as he speaks. "You are leaving tomorrow," he says. "The tenement block is being emptied."

We all stare at him for a moment. Vati is first to break the silence. "Leaving to go where?" he asks.

"It's a good place," the man says. "You will all stay together. All the families. It's a safe place. They have assured us of this."

He looks up at us, and I notice his eyes are glistening. I wonder for a second if he sleeps well at night, or if he lies awake, troubled by his job. A messenger for the Nazis. But that is all he is, just a messenger. He doesn't make the rules, and he will no doubt be discarded like the rest of us when he's served his purpose.

"I'm sorry," he says. "I do not know any more than that."

Vati pats him on the arm. "Hey, it's all right. It's not your fault."

The man nods gratefully. "You can each bring one suitcase," he goes on. "They will be here early."

The other fathers step forward to talk further with the man. The mothers gather the children together. I feel like a baby bird, small and helpless, unable to look after myself, to eat, to fly.

Greta touches my arm. "Elsa, I need to get back to my parents." Her eyes have lost their sparkle and her face is gray.

"Of course. I—I'll see you in the morning."

We hug briefly and then she leaves. The *Judenrat* man leaves shortly after her, and I go to our room.

Mutti is already in there starting to tidy and pack up our things. I grab the bags from beside the grubby mattress that the four of us have shared since we came to live here.

Amid the fear and panic and sudden rush of activity, one thought brings me a twisted kind of comfort: we own so little now that at least it won't take long to pack.

Max

"One, two, three, go!" Max slammed his hand down on his knee, fingers spread in a V shape.

"I win! I got the scissors!" He pointed at the other boy's hand, his palm flat on its side. "You lose, Erich."

The boys were at the park for a Hitler Youth afternoon. Erich was one of Max's Hitler Youth friends. He wasn't Max's *best* friend. To be honest, Max wasn't sure which of them he would call his best friend. Probably none of them. He didn't need a best friend anyway. He served Hitler. That was all he needed.

The other boys would be here soon for a rally and training, but Erich and Max had arrived early and decided to play their favorite game while they waited: Soldiers.

"Best of three!" Erich said. He put both palms together, in a mock begging action. "Please! I always lose. It's not fair!"

Max laughed. "You always lose because I am better than you," he teased.

Erich stuck his elbow out to nudge Max in the side, but Max swerved out of his way. "See. You can't get me. I'm better than you at everything."

Erich jumped up. "We'll see about that," he said.

Max was on his toes in a second. "Come on, then," he said. "If you can catch me before I get to the end of the field, you get to choose who's who. If you can't, I do. Fair?"

Erich shrugged. "Fair," he said.

"Okay. Go!" Max ran as fast as he could across the field. Erich was right behind him, maybe an arm's length away. As Max fought to stay ahead of his friend, something about it felt familiar. Running like this, playing chase in the park. How many times had he done this with Leo? Too many to count.

The thought of it flashed a pain across his chest. He sped up even more, so that he could outrun the memory.

Max reached the end of the field two seconds before Erich. "Loser!" Max said, laughing as the two boys panted and fell to the ground.

"Okay. Fair enough," Erich said. "You win. You get to choose."

Max didn't have to think about his decision. "I'll be the Nazi soldier."

"Of course you will," Erich said dejectedly.

Max stood and mimed putting a steel helmet on his head. As he did so, he could almost feel himself becoming a real soldier. He filled his lungs with air, puffed out his chest, and stuck out his jaw.

Then he pointed at Erich, still sitting on the ground. "*Sieg heil!*" he shouted. "Get up! Lazy Jew!"

Erich held his hands up in front of him and laughed. "Hey, all right, all right. I'm getting up," he said. "I didn't realize we'd started playing."

Max was firmly in his role before Erich had even stopped laughing. He shouted even louder this time. "Get up! NOW!" He felt the soldier inside him fizzing through his veins. Max tried to remind himself it *was* a game. But to him it was so much more. It was training. It was preparation. It was enacting the words that he said out loud in front of the mirror each morning. The speech that every member of the Hitler Youth knew by heart.

The German boy of the future must be slender and supple, as swift as a greyhound, as tough as leather, and as hard as Krupp's steel.

Those words guided Max's actions and defined his ambitions. Next year he and Erich would join the senior ranks of the Hitler Youth, and Max could hardly wait to take everything he had learned to the next level. Games like this were his chance to hone his skills to the finest point possible, prove himself to his father—and to Hitler.

Erich dragged himself off the ground. "Sorry, sir," he said, standing up and straightening his jacket.

"March!" Max barked at his friend, almost spitting the words out. "Now!"

Erich sloped across the field. As he walked, he bent a finger in front of his face in the shape of a massive hooked nose, just like the Jewish caricatures on the Nazi posters that lined every wall of their city. Every now and then, he stopped to hold his arms out in a wide, exaggerated shrug. "Oh, poor me. I'm a dirty Jew," he'd say. "I am a despicable human being. I am worse than a human being. I am a dog, a rat. I am a stain on society."

The way he did it was so over the top that Max couldn't help laughing. Then he shook himself and got back into his role. "Come on," he said, giving Erich a prod. "Keep marching."

Max taunted and shouted and called his friend names all the way across the field. And with every step and with each insult he hurled, he felt waves of relief flood over him that he had won the race.

Erich looked so dejected by the time they reached the other side, Max wasn't sure if his friend was playing his own part well or if Max had made such a good job of playing soldier that Erich was genuinely fed up.

But Max knew one thing: he would do all he could possibly do to make sure he was always the one who got to make the decisions in this game.

There was no way he would ever be the filthy Jew.

Elsa

ome on, come on, we haven't got all day."

The soldiers shout and curse at us as we file out of our buildings and into the street. There must be over a thousand of us: old, young, couples, families. It's not a military operation, but the guards are acting as if it should be.

We are soon squashed together so tightly we have to coordinate our movements with each other to make any progress. An elderly couple in front of me are shuffling along so slowly that a woman behind me keeps walking into me and catching my heels with her case.

"I'm sorry, I'm sorry," she says.

"It's fine. Honestly, don't worry," Mutti says to her on my behalf. I'm too busy looking down at my feet, concentrating on my next step, to be able to turn around and speak to her myself.

We are approaching the edge of our small neighborhood. We haven't been allowed past this point for months now. As we near the corner to the outside world, a guard is screaming at everyone who passes. "Get back in line! Turn left! Pick your feet up! Keep moving!"

To underline his orders, he uses the end of his rifle to prod people as they come past him. I am terrified he will point his rifle at me, so I double my speed, even if it means I am shoving the old couple in front of me.

We get past the guard without incident. And then we are in a wide street. Mutti, Vati, Otto, and I—a line of four in among the thousand other ragged, dirty, tired, confused people shuffling along beside us.

Otto is holding on to his leg. His limp has been worse than ever recently.

"Are you all right?" I ask him.

He nods. "I'm fine. Honestly." He gives me a weak smile.

"Lean on me if you need to, okay?"

"I will."

Just then I hear a familiar voice. "Elsa!" I spin round to see Greta turning the corner and coming out onto the street. She grabs her mother's arm and drags her parents over to join us. As soon as she is beside me, we clutch hands and a tiny bit of my fear melts away. As long as I have my best friend beside me, I will be all right.

"Did you feed Felix?" I ask her.

Greta nods. "He came to our apartment before the sun was up. I think he must have known we were leaving. I gave him half my dinner from last night. I'd been saving it for him."

"I can't believe we have to leave him," I say.

"I know. Maybe he'll find us," Greta replies brightly. "I'm sure we'll get to see him again."

I don't know if she really believes it, but the thought of him padding along, following us to wherever we're going, cheers me a little.

"Move!" one of the guards yells so suddenly it makes me jump. "Go!"

The group lumbers on down the road. We are somewhere around the middle, and now that we are in this wide street, people have begun to spread out enough that at least we can walk without bumping into anyone.

Soldiers march along on both sides of us. There seem to be more of them than ever this morning. All wearing rifles over their shoulders, swastika bands on their arms, and the fiercest expressions on their faces.

They glance into the crowd, barking at people as we walk. Instinctively Greta and I stop talking, keep looking ahead, and walk as briskly as we can. We've learned how we have to act in order to not draw attention to ourselves.

After what feels like hours of walking, my legs are tired. I want to stop and rest. I need water, and my stomach is growling for food. But I daren't say anything. I saw a man a few rows ahead of us ask if he could stop a little while ago, and one of the guards grabbed him by his arm and dragged him away. I don't know where they took him. I didn't dare look. But it was enough to make sure I won't be stopping to ask for *anything*.

Eventually the pace starts to slow. We're approaching the train station, and as we get closer, we can see that people seem to be gathering in a group up ahead.

"It's the old junkyard," Vati says, in a low voice so the guards won't scream at him for talking.

"What are we going there for?" Otto asks.

"I have no idea," Mutti replies. As we get closer, we see a line of long tables with all sorts of things on them. It reminds me of the square in Vienna on market days.

The guards push us and prod us and direct us to file past the tables. People are stopping in front of them in groups of twenty or so at a time.

When our turn comes, SS guards stand all around us. "Open your cases here!" one of them shouts. "Anything valuable goes on the table. Necklaces, bracelets, rings—all of it on these tables."

The four of us look at each other. Mutti's face has drained of color. "What does he mean?" she hisses. "What valuables do we still have, even? Have they not already taken everything we own? My life is in this one bag. I have *nothing* valuable!"

Vati puts his hand on Mutti's arm. He strokes her finger. "My darling," he says, his voice croaking as if it is filled with sawdust, "we must give him your ring."

Mutti makes a sobbing sound that comes out as though she is

210

choking. "My wedding ring? It is not enough that these Nazis have taken our home, our possessions, our lives, our dignity? They must have the symbol of our love as well?"

"I will buy you another one, I promise you. When this is all over, I will put a band of gold around your finger and it will stay there forever, with my love."

Mutti doesn't say anything. But eventually she nods and silently begins to tug the ring from her finger.

At that moment, one of the SS guards pulls a man out of the line, seemingly for no reason, and drags him into a shed behind the tables. We hear the sounds of a scuffle, the man crying out.

I clap my hand over my mouth. The salty taste of bile is in my throat, and I don't know if I can stop myself from being sick. Each time I think they have treated us as horribly as they can, somehow the guards manage to do something even worse.

For a moment I am grateful that we have barely eaten in days. At least I have nothing to bring up.

A few moments later, the man is dragged out of the shed. His left eye is closed and already swelling. He's limping. He has blood dripping from his forehead.

"This is what happens if you try to hide anything!" the officer shouts to us as he lets go of the man. He stumbles back into the crowd.

My mouth is as dry as the gravelly path under our feet. What if I have something in my bag that I don't realize is valuable? What if I forget it or miss it and they take me to the shed and—

"Come on, children, hurry," Vati says, breaking into my terrified thoughts. "Just look through your things and make sure there is nothing they might want."

I scrabble through my bag. There is nothing in here. Nothing of any value. At least not to the SS men anyway. My hand grazes the thing of most value to me, besides the people I am with: the photograph of me, Leo, and Max. The memory of that day still shines a light inside me, and I cannot bear to give it away. To anyone else, it is a fading photograph, a torn scrap of paper. The Nazis would not want this. But I also can't risk them finding something so precious to me.

I fold it into a cardigan to keep it hidden as I finish rifling through my clothes. "Nothing," I say.

The guard behind the table gives me a sharp nod. "Close it. You are done," he says before moving on to check Otto's bag.

I close my bag and turn to see where Mutti and Vati are. In front of them on the table, Mutti's wedding ring and Vati's gold watch sit next to each other. The guard grabs them and drops them in a box by his side. "Go," he says to my parents.

Wordlessly they close their bags and turn away from the table. The four of us shuffle into the crowd as the next group lines up to hand over their last remaining valuables.

We are directed toward the train station by the guards. I look for Greta in the crowds. We've become separated, and a tiny sliver of panic starts to creep into my chest until I spot her, near the platform. A large train is waiting, and people are being shoved and pushed into carriages.

There she is! Standing outside one of the carriages with her parents. "Greta! Wait for me!" I shout.

She turns and sees me, but a second later, a guard pushes her forward and she is forced to get into the carriage.

I pull on Mutti's sleeve. "Hurry, please. We must get into the same carriage as Greta."

"Okay, we'll try," Mutti replies, but there are still too many people in front of us and we are pushed onto the next one instead.

Mutti grips my hand. "You'll see her when we get there," she says. "Let's stay together for now."

She's doing that thing she does so often nowadays: trying to sound calm and normal, but I know she feels far from either. I hear the quiver that runs through every word, and I know not to argue. Instead I squeeze her hand, and keep hold of it.

"Where are we going, anyway?" Otto asks. "Why won't they tell us?"

One of the guards overhears him and flashes a cold smile in our direction. "You have nothing to worry about," he says. "You're being taken somewhere safe to keep you away from the stresses of war."

"Where?" a brave man shouts. "Where is this safe place you are taking us?"

For a moment, there is silence as everyone in the carriage holds their breath, waiting to see what will happen. Will this man be taken out and beaten for daring to question the guards? Or will we actually get an answer?

It seems he is in luck, and so are we, as the guard smiles and answers mildly, "It is a nice place. A new ghetto especially for you lucky Jews. It's called Theresienstadt. You will be happy there. You will like it. We will look after you there."

I remember what the man from the Jewish Council said last night. Is it true? Are they helping us?

I can't stop myself wanting to believe him. A tiny flame of optimism glimmers like a flickering candle in the dark. Can I let myself believe he is telling the truth? Are they really looking after us at last? Do they finally see how unfair everyone is to the Jews and they are giving us a chance to live our lives in peace? Maybe there will be a park we can walk in! We'll be able to go to school, ride bicycles, maybe even sleep in our own beds instead of sharing a dirty mattress between four of us.

Can I dare to let myself dream even for a few minutes?

I know I shouldn't, but the guard's words are so reassuring I can't stop myself. Now I just want to get moving, but people are still clambering aboard the train.

Our carriage is full, and still more and more people pile inside. So many people that soon we can barely move.

A feeling of panic swirls in my stomach.

And then the doors finally close and the last bit of air is shut out. We are sealed in. I think back to science class—although it feels like a lifetime ago that I had lessons, that I went to school. I remember learning about oxygen. We need it to breathe, to live. How much do we need? Is there enough in here? All these people breathing. In and out. In and out. Using up the oxygen. What happens to us after it's gone?

I realize my mind is racing so fast that the thoughts no longer make sense.

"Mutti," I croak. I haven't got enough room to twist my body, so I can't look for her.

"I'm here, darling," she whispers from behind me.

"I'm here, too," Vati says from somewhere else.

"And me," Otto's voice adds from even further away.

All around me, people are doing the same. We are like animals in the wild, bleating and crying to find our families. Bleating and crying to those we love, calling out names as we stand here waiting, waiting, waiting.

And then there is a sudden jerk. As one, we fall. Bodies moving against bodies, rolling forward, then back again.

Slowly the train clanks into movement. We settle into a jagged rhythm, swaying together, gripping arms of people we cannot even see, pressing feet and knees against people we hardly know.

As we rock and sway and breathe each other's breath in and out, sharing the air as if it were a prize in a game of pass the parcel, I find myself noticing how easy it is for something absurd to become almost natural.

How rapidly something unthinkable can become commonplace. How easily we let the inconceivable become a new normal.

215

How quickly we learn to stop questioning these things.

And amid all these thoughts, I find myself wondering if we will at last find our way back to some kind of life when we get to Theresienstadt.

I don't want to wish for it. I should know by now that dreams no longer come true. But I can't stop myself. I allow myself the luxury of hope.

1942

Max

The cold February day was here at last. It seemed to Max he'd been waiting his whole life for this day.

His fourteenth birthday and the day he progressed from the junior section of the Hitler Youth to the real thing.

His father had organized a party for him that evening. Max could barely concentrate on his schoolwork all day. Luckily, his teachers understood. Everyone knew the pride he was feeling, the hunger to give himself fully and completely to the *Führer*, to know that from this day onward he was not a boy, an individual, a someone. He was part of the regime: a soldier who would take his part in spreading the message of the Aryan race and commit his life to fighting Germany's enemies.

He would no longer have to settle for sports days and weekend camps. Now the real training would begin. He would be learning the things that really mattered. Bayonet drill, grenade-throwing, trench-digging, map-reading, pistol-shooting, how to get under barbed wire. These things would be his life from this moment on, and nothing else mattered.

Every fiber of his being itched with the desire to take his place and give himself to Hitler.

Finally the school day was over and he was back home waiting for the party to begin.

The doorbell rang at six on the dot. Max opened the door for his friends and stood to attention, ready to greet them.

"*Heil Hitler!*" the three boys said in unison at the top of the stairs.

Max snapped his heels together. His face solemn and composed, he raised his arm in a proud salute. "*Heil Hitler!*" he shouted back to them.

His mother had made tea for the boys, and they crowded around the dining room table to eat. The boys looked identical, with their combed and parted hair, their spotless uniforms and swastika armbands.

"Look at you all, so handsome and so grown-up," his mother said as they ate.

"The boys do not care about being handsome!" his father scoffed, wiping his mouth and folding his napkin back into a perfect square. "That is not why they look smart. They do it because they care about order, discipline, and obedience." He turned to his son. "Am I right?"

Max nodded sharply. "Yes, sir," he said.

"Well, I think it's all right for a mother to think her son looks handsome," Mrs. Fischer replied as she picked up their empty plates and took them to the sink.

Once her back was turned, Max's father nudged him, and with the tiniest hint of a smile, he rolled his eyes. "Women, eh?" he said in a conspiratorial sort of manner that filled Max's heart.

His mother came back to the table with Max's birthday cake. It was a Black Forest gateau.

Max's friends gasped. "That looks wonderful, Mrs. Fischer," one of them, Heinrich, said. "How did you get all those ingredients in wartime?"

Mrs. Fischer laughed and pointed to her husband. "Being married to a senior SS officer has its uses," she said.

The boys all laughed in reply. Even Mr. Fischer cracked a wry smile.

It was the best evening Max could remember having. Ever.

Except for ... maybe one other evening. One time when the Black Forest gateau would have been a Viennese Sachertorte. When the tight discipline would have been replaced by carefree running around in a carriage high in the air. When the polite laughter was instead wide smiles captured in a photograph that he had not looked at or even thought about for years.

Stop.

What was he doing? What was he thinking? How could he insult his parents by even allowing a tiny part of his mind to go there?

Max forced himself back into the present moment. And for the rest of the evening he made sure to show his mother how much he adored her cake: the best he had *ever* eaten. He ensured he did nothing to anger his father. Max was the most generous and delightful host he could possibly be to his friends.

It was *definitely* the best birthday, he was absolutely sure of it.

But still, at the end of the evening, when the other boys had left and Max had helped his mother wash and dry the plates and his father had lit a fire in the lounge where he sat with a book, something tugged at a corner of Max's mind. The corner that could not quite let go of that other birthday party.

He took himself off to his bedroom and opened his wardrobe. Kneeling down, he reached to the back for the shoebox he hadn't opened since they had moved to Munich. He scrabbled through shoes and bags and mothballs that had never seen the light of day. And then ...

There! He pulled the shoebox out, his arms doing the work without stopping to consult his mind. If they had, they would surely have known better.

He sat on the side of his bed and took the lid off the box. As he opened it, a smell of something from inside it climbed into Max's heart. What was it? The books? The photographs? The old teddy bear he had completely forgotten about? It was hard to say, but the smell took him straight back to Vienna.

He closed his eyes, and he could see it all. Leo and Elsa and him. Running, playing tag, riding their bikes, diving into the

Amalienbad, always talking, always teasing, *always* smiling.

The feeling was so intense Max wouldn't even call it a memory. It was stronger than that. He was *there*. And it hurt. It hurt so much. It ripped into his skin, scorching down into his being. The outer layers fell away. In an instant, nothing of his current life was real. He saw it for what it was: a vain, superficial attempt to fit in. To be loved. To be praised by his father, by his leaders, by Hitler. None of it was a fraction as real as his friendships with Leo and Elsa had been. The only two people who had ever really loved him for himself, with no expectations or demands.

Max's heart hurt so much he found himself clutching his chest with one hand as he rummaged through the box with the other. And then he found what he'd been looking for.

The photo. The smiles. The linked arms.

And he was suddenly back there in that carriage, transported as if on a flying carpet to that wonderful, magical—

"What are you doing?"

His father was at the door. His frame filled the doorway and blotted out the light behind him.

"I . . ."

Max shoved the photo back into the box, but his father had crossed the room in two strides and was towering over him, holding out his hand. "Show me," he said.

Max knew better than to do anything other than obey. He handed the photo to his father. And then he looked at the floor and waited for the onslaught of rage.

It didn't come. Max raised his eyes to look up. His father studied the photo, nodding slowly, and then he handed it back to Max.

"Why were you looking at this?" he asked calmly. Too calmly.

"I just ... I ..." Max paused. In the pause, he knew what he had to do. He had to use this moment to strengthen his will. Of *course* he remembered his old friends on his birthday. It was only natural. But they weren't his friends now. They were nothing to him. They were a thing from another lifetime, as was that day. They were not real friends, not like the friends he had now. They were *Jews*. He knew that now. He accepted it now. They could never be his friends.

Max realized what this moment was all about. His memories had led him here as a challenge, a test. This was truly the moment where he had reached the fork in the road. He could hanker after long-forgotten laughs and childish games, or he could push himself past all of that emotion and make the commitment that today demanded of him.

He knew what he had to do.

"I was looking for the photograph so that I could destroy it," Max said evenly.

His father stared at him for a moment. The darkness in his eyes was like a black hole, and Max thought he might be swallowed up in it forever if he wasn't careful. Finally, after an age, his father nodded again, then turned his back. "Come," he said sharply. "And bring the photograph."

Still holding the photo, Max jumped up from his bed and followed his father out of the room.

At the door to the lounge, Mr. Fischer hesitated. "Wait in there," he said, pointing into the room. "I'll be back in a moment."

Max waited as he heard his father enter his office, the room next to the lounge. In the silence, he held the photo so tightly his palm had begun to sweat. He forced himself not to look at it again.

A minute or two later, his father was back in the room. He had something in his hand. A huge bundle of paper, wrapped in string.

He held it out to Max. "Here, take these," he said.

Max took the bundle and turned it over in his hands. It was a pile of envelopes. There must have been twenty or thirty of them. But why . . .

"Look at them," his father instructed, folding his arms as he watched Max's face.

Max pulled out a couple of the envelopes—and immediately realized what they were. He knew that handwriting. He had sat next to the boy who formed those spindly letters every day at school in Vienna.

They were letters from Leo. Letters he had never received, never seen, never known existed.

Max's chest tightened as he fought the urge to rip the envelopes open and consume what was inside them.

He knew what was expected of him.

Feeling his father's eyes boring into him, Max walked to the fireplace. He held the envelopes out. Hesitated. Took a breath.

"Go on," his father said softly.

Max felt a tear sneaking into the corner of his eye. No. He wouldn't let it out. He hardened his will. This was the challenge that would truly make him a man. *This* was his birthday gift from his father.

The memory of his old friends was the final thing he had to let go of. Once he had cut that tie, once he had proved that Hitler and the Nazi regime meant more to him than anything else, there would be nothing in his way. He could give himself in his heart, body, mind, and spirit to the party and his country—and once he'd done that, he knew he could conquer anything.

He threw the letters into the fire. The flames curled around the envelopes, greedy and starving, turning Leo's words to ash.

Max still had the photograph. The final link to the boy he could never be again.

Without hesitating for another second, he held the photo out in front of him, and threw it onto the fire.

His father put a hand on his shoulder. Max could not remember a single time in his life when he had felt his father's touch, and the sensation made him dizzy.

"Good man," Mr. Fischer said.

Good man? His father had called him a man? *Now* he knew what true happiness was. Now he knew his real purpose in life. Now he was a soldier.

Together, they watched the flames. The photograph hissed and curled; the childish smiles melted into nothing. Max stood tall and proud beside his father as a door in his heart silently closed.

Leo

We had a new geography teacher at school today. Mrs. Whitehead. And something quite amazing happened.

We each had to stand up and go to the front of the class in turn. Mrs. Whitehead had placed a big map on the board, and we had to point to a country and tell her something about it.

It was my turn to go up. I told myself we'd lived here over two years and there was no reason to worry. The boys no longer bullied me. Sure, we still played soldiers most of the time, and sometimes some of the things they said made me wince. But I didn't *always* have to play the German nowadays. And they didn't say "*Sieg heil*" and laugh at me anymore.

I didn't go out of my way to talk about being Jewish, but I didn't go out of my way to hide it either. Daniel had helped with that.

Just knowing I had an ally, even if we never really talked about it, made me feel more normal, more like one of the boys.

So I decided to be brave.

I pointed at Austria and said that it was where I was born. For a second, it all came back. Those last months in Vienna. I'd pushed it all so far away from me, it was like remembering someone else's life. Someone else's mother crouched in the cupboard while shops and houses were smashed up; someone else's father taken away by his friends. Someone else who had nightmares every single night for the first year of living in England.

But it wasn't someone else; it was me. And while I stood there at the front of the class, I remembered that other day, when I was made to stand up in front of the whole school.

I could feel my knees about to buckle as a feeling of nausea crept into my throat. Maybe I'd been kidding myself about being normal here, about being safe. In that moment, part of me still expected the teacher to point at me and call me names, and the other kids to turn and stare silently as I walked to the back of the room.

Mrs. Whitehead's voice brought me back to the present moment. "Really?" she asked. "You must have left when you were a baby?"

I shook my head and swallowed down my fears and my memories. "It was just over two years ago," I said. "I was twelve."

Her eyes went all wide and she said, "I never would have guessed. You sound perfectly English to me."

I walked back to my seat almost in a trance. Daniel gave me

a nudge and smiled at me. "See," he whispered. He still had to tell me on a regular basis that I had nothing to worry about.

Maybe he was right. Maybe I *could* dare to believe it.

I sounded "perfectly English."

I found myself breaking into a smile. It didn't leave my face for the rest of the day. All day, I could feel myself walk a little taller, laugh a little harder, join in a little more.

I was *perfectly English*. I was no longer an outsider.

And yes, sometimes I wondered if I would ever get to see Vienna again, and I knew that it would always have a special place in my heart. But England was where I lived now, and it seemed that, at last, I could let myself think of it as home.

I floated on air through the rest of the lesson, and on into the next. Science with Mr. Rogers.

We had barely started the lesson when we heard a familiar sound outside the classroom. The siren. Air raid.

Usually it was a drill, to make sure we knew what to do, but you never knew for sure, and it had been drummed into us that we were to act as if it were real every single time.

"Tom, Sally, Peter, fetch the gas masks from the cloakroom. Leo, Daniel, and Mary, help hand them out. The rest of you line up by the door. When everyone has their gas mask, take it with you and let's go."

I hurried to do my job as quickly as possible. In less than two minutes, the whole class had their gas masks and had formed a line at the door.

"Good," Mr. Rogers said. "Right, come on."

We followed Mr. Rogers out into the corridor and joined the children coming out of all the other classrooms. We filled the corridor and hurried out to the yard.

The headmaster, Mr. Salisbury, was outside directing us to the shelters. They'd only been built two years ago, especially for us in case there was an actual raid while we were at school.

"Is it real or a drill, sir?" a boy from another class asked as we passed him.

"It's a drill this time," he answered. "But remember, we treat it exactly the same as we would if it were real."

I hurried across the yard with my classmates, then down a narrow tunnel and into the underground cave where we would spend at least the rest of the lesson. The longest we'd had to spend in there was two hours. That was the one time it was real.

"What are you doing at the weekend?" Daniel asked as we squashed together on the concrete bench.

I shrugged. "Helping Mom, I guess."

We'd moved out of the Stewarts' house last year. Mama—or "Mom" as I called her in front of my friends—had said we couldn't abuse their kindness any longer, especially now that the war and rationing meant things were tough for all of us. We'd been living with them for over a year so it was quite a change—but she was right. It was time we started to be independent.

She'd found a tiny flat for us. She had the bedroom; I slept on a sofa in the lounge. It wasn't perfect, but at least it was our own place.

The wallpaper was about fifty years old and peeling off, and when we moved in, Mr. Stewart had said that we had to replace it.

Mama had laughed. "Where do you expect me to get wallpaper?" she asked. "It's hard enough to find butter for my bread and sugar for my tea nowadays. Wallpaper is a luxury I don't expect to find until the war is over!"

Mr. Stewart had frowned. "I'll find you some," he'd said. "I'm not letting you live like this. My wife would not forgive me."

It took a while but he'd been true to his word, and just last week he'd brought round three rolls of wallpaper with big green and blue flowers on it. I'd promised Mama I would help put it up this weekend.

"Too bad," Daniel said to me now. "Rory says he's going to take us to the cinema."

Rory was the American soldier Daniel's older sister Maddy had started going out with. It had pretty much made Daniel the most popular boy in the class. Rory was always bringing Daniel's family things that were nearly impossible to find now. Coffee, evaporated milk; last week he'd even brought them sugar, and Daniel's mom had made a cake with it. Daniel brought a piece into school for me. It had nothing on the Sachertorte Mama used to make, but compared to the basic food we had to eat now, it was heavenly!

But the cinema! That was a special treat. "What film are you going to see?"

"*Bambi.*"

"What's that?"

Daniel pulled a face. "It's about a baby deer and his friends. Sounds like a kids' film really. It's on in the morning."

"Really? Okay, I'll see if Mom will agree to start wallpapering in the afternoon. Count me in!"

The next day, I finished off my breakfast, cleared my plate, and went over to say goodbye to Mama. "You sure you're all right with me going out?" I asked.

She patted my hand. "Of course, darling. I'll make something nice for lunch, and then we'll get started this afternoon."

I kissed her on the cheek. "Thanks, Mama."

Daniel was in the line at the cinema with his sister and Rory. I went over to join them. "Oi!" someone said pointedly from behind us as I shuffled into the line.

I turned around to see two girls I vaguely recognized from school. The one who'd spoken had long blond hair and big green eyes that she fixed on me. "That's pushing in!" she said. The other girl pulled her dark hair over her face and blushed as I glanced at her.

"I—I'm really sorry," I said to them both. "I'll go to the back if you like."

The blond girl shrugged. "It's okay," she said, a twinkle in her eye. "We just wanted to get your attention. Been trying for weeks." Then she nudged her friend. "Haven't we, Annie?"

Annie's face flushed an even deeper shade of red as she looked at me from under her bangs. Her eyes were dark brown, and she turned them away from me too quickly. I wanted her to look at me again. My mouth had gone dry, and all the words I knew seemed to have deserted me.

"Why don't you ladies join us?" Rory burst in, smiling his smooth, wide smile that I was pretty sure all the girls loved as much as his US army uniform. "I'll treat you, to make up for my friend here line-jumping. Sit with us."

They gave each other a quick look, like they were speaking a secret language that only girls understood. Something about the movement reminded me of Elsa. The sharing of secrets, the sweetness of the smiles, the idea of being close to a girl again. I found myself holding my breath while I waited for them to reply.

Then, with another shrug and in a voice that was probably meant to sound casual but didn't fool anyone, the blond girl said, "Sure. Why not?"

As we shuffled along in the line, I soon realized that Annie was walking along next to me. "I'm Leo," I said awkwardly.

"I'm Annie," she said.

I reached out to shake her hand. "Hi," I mumbled.

She looked at my hand and, with a soft laugh, reached out and shook it.

I wanted to keep holding her hand, but the moment passed and soon we were at the front of the line and then we were inside in the darkness—and I found I could barely breathe as she sat down next to me.

I barely watched the film. All I knew was that every now and then, I could feel Annie's arm brushing mine. One time, we both had our hands on the armrest and I could feel the back of her fingers against mine. I didn't move a muscle. I'm not sure I even breathed for a few minutes.

"I—I'll see you at school," I said when we parted after the film.

Annie smiled at me. "I hope so," she replied, and my heart leaped out of my body, twirled around a lamppost a few times, and jumped back in again.

Daniel ribbed me about it all the way home. "Leo's got a girl-friend, Leo's got a girlfriend," he sang.

Rory and Maddy laughed. "Leave him alone," Maddy said.

But I didn't mind. It wasn't like the days when the boys called me names that made me feel like crawling into a ball. This was being teased by my friend and I was too full of happiness to care. And besides, I quite liked the idea that Annie might possibly be my girlfriend.

I got home and let myself into the flat.

Mama was standing in the middle of the kitchen, and there were scraps of wallpaper in her hair and all over the floor, the chairs—everywhere but on the walls, it seemed.

She turned to face me, a wire brush in her hand, and smiled. "I've made a start," she said.

I rolled up my sleeves. "I'll join you," I said.

"Let's have lunch first. You can tell me all about the film, and then we'll get to work."

I told her as much as I could remember about the film. I didn't mention anything else, though. I wouldn't have known how to put it into words.

After lunch, I put on my scruffiest clothes and joined Mama in the kitchen. We worked all afternoon and into the evening, chatting and laughing and scraping and scrubbing at the walls.

I think it was the best day I'd had since we'd come to England.

As the room began to darken, we stopped working and cleared a space on the table. Mama lit a special candle and said the havdalah prayer for the end of Shabbat. Then she kissed me on the cheek.

Our Saturdays were so different now—almost indistinguishable from any other day. But still, the havdalah prayer reminded me where we'd come from, and who we still were. And those things would never change.

It was too early for dinner. "Shall we do a bit more before we eat?" I asked.

"If you're happy to. Let's have a little music while we work, shall we?" Mama switched on the radio, and we got back to our work, humming along with some of the tunes.

When Vera Lynn came on, Mama stopped humming, stopped scraping, and sat down in one of the chairs, now randomly placed in the middle of the room and covered in bits of wallpaper.

"*We'll meet again . . .* ," Vera Lynn sang.

"Don't know where, don't know when," Mama sang along with

her. Suddenly her voice cracked and her shoulders started shaking as she dropped her head.

I stopped scraping and went over to her. Her eyes were red, lines of tears carving wet trails through the wallpaper dust on her cheeks.

Seeing her upset made me want to cry too, and the joy of my day dissolved at her tears, and at the cause of them—the fact that Papa wasn't here. More than anything, I wanted to sob my heart out, wail like a child, have her comfort me and tell me everything was going to be all right.

And then I remembered what Papa had said to me. I found it harder and harder to fully remember his face now, but his words from the dark day when they took him away had never left me.

You are the man of the house now. You look after your mother. You hear me? You promise me?

I put my wire brush on the floor and crouched down in front of Mama, reaching out to lift her chin.

"Mama," I said. She looked at me through damp, dark eyes. "We *will* see Papa again. I promise you."

"I just miss him so much," she said. "I can't bear it. Never knowing where he is, what has become of him. I try not to think the worst but—"

"No." I stopped her. "We must never think like that. One day Papa will walk into this place and he'll say, 'What on earth is that crooked paper you have all over the walls?' and then you will dance together in this very kitchen."

Mama laughed softly. "My darling boy, I hope and pray you are right."

I wiped her cheek with my thumb. "I am, Mama. I promise you."

She clutched my hand. "You are such a good boy," she said. Then she shook her head. "No. You are such a good *man*. My wonderful young man. The best thing in my life."

I reached out to put my arms around her waist. She leaned her head against me and stroked my hair.

And behind us, Vera Lynn sang out.

"*Keep smiling through, just like you always do. . . . I know we'll meet again some sunny day.*"

Elsa

I'm riding in some sort of train carriage. I know I've been here before but I can't remember when. I'm packed in with so many people that I can barely breathe. It all feels familiar. So familiar. But then the carriage rises from its tracks, climbing up into the air, and the doors open and we look out over the city.

Max and Leo are with me. Their bodies on either side of me keep me warm. Our friendship wraps me in a bubble of happiness.

"Elsa!"

At the sound of my name, Max and Leo are suddenly moving away.

No! Don't go. Stay close to me. Keep me warm. Don't leave me!

Someone is shaking me. "Elsa!" The voice is insistent. "Elsa, wake up!"

And then I realize. I've been dreaming.

The disappointment is so crushing it feels like an actual weight on my body. Max and Leo aren't here at all. They haven't been here for longer than I can remember. Their existence itself feels like a dream. I don't want to open my eyes.

"Elsa, you have to get up. They'll be here for roll call soon."

Eventually I force myself to open my eyes. Mutti's face is inches away from mine. "Elsa, please." Her voice is feverish. "There is another transport today. In the night, three women in our block received a summons. We can't give them any reason to add us to the list."

"Mutti, I'm sorry. I'm up, I promise."

I pull the thin rag that passes for a blanket off my body and swing my legs round to get off the bunk. I barely notice the aches and pains that come from a night of sleeping on such an uncomfortable bed. After nearly a year at Theresienstadt, I am used to the aches, and mostly they are the least of my troubles.

I have no memories of a time before this—in my waking hours, anyway.

I don't remember nights before these ones, during which Mutti and I share a bunk bed so narrow that if one of us wants to turn over in the night, the other must mirror their movements or risk falling onto the floor.

I don't remember ever having anything over my body at night other than a blanket that's so dirty I have no idea what color it was before this murky gray, and so torn that the holes take up more space than the material itself.

I don't remember a time when my thoughts involved more than wondering if I will find enough to eat so that my stomach won't growl and cramp and buckle all day long.

Is it any wonder I prefer to dream?

We join the others outside in the square.

Greta finds me, and she and her mother stand with us.

"Okay?" Greta asks, stroking my hair like she always does.

I smile softly at her. "Okay," I reply, and reach out to squeeze her hand. "You?"

"Better now," she says, squeezing my hand back.

As always, I search around for Vati and Otto. We haven't seen them for over a week. The men's camps are quite close, really. But my father and brother might as well be on another continent, for all the chance we have of seeing them.

Yesterday two men were caught sending letters to their wives. The soldiers told us they would be punished today.

We are all here, standing in the cold, waiting for the daily orders, when the men are dragged out in front of us.

"See this?" a guard shouts. "This is how we treat those who think they are cleverer than us!"

And then he pulls out a huge whip. He orders one of the men to bend down.

The man is crying. "Please. Please, no." His hands are held together in prayer. He kneels at the guard's feet. "I beg you."

In reply, the guard kicks him in the stomach so hard that the man almost flies through the air and lands on his side. The guard

241

kicks him again so that the man flops over onto his front, his face in the dirt.

And then the guard uses the whip on him.

The other guard holds on to the second man and screams at us, "Anyone who looks away will face the same punishment!"

No one looks away. A couple of people are sick on the ground right in front of where they stand. I bunch my fist into my mouth to make sure that doesn't happen to me.

When you live on one bowl of thin soup a day, you need to keep it all down.

Luckily for me, Mutti is one of the kitchen helpers, which means that sometimes she manages to sneak away some kind of treasure. Last week she came to the barracks with a whole potato! We could hardly believe it. She cut it into six portions and shared it with the women in our corner of the barrack.

I made my portion last two whole days. And that included giving half of it to Greta.

Greta is my lifeline. I don't think I could survive here without her. We don't play like we used to. We don't gossip and tease each other. But we still talk. We still dream. We still pretend to plan a life after this. We still smile. We smile sometimes.

We made a rule a few weeks ago. Every day we have to find something good to say. Every single day, something new. We have managed it so far. I try to recall at least five of them each day, and I say them to myself whenever the guards shout at us.

It feels like a rebellion.

I do it now, as the guards whip the two men. But it doesn't feel like rebellion today. Rebellion feels like far too ambitious an idea. Remembering the good things feels like survival.

I fill my mind as much as I can, trying to drown out the sounds of the men's screams.

One: The potato. The thought of it makes my mouth water, even now.

Two: I have Mutti, we are together.

Three: I have Greta. That's two people who love me, who I see every single day. It's more than most people have now.

Four: We heard from Vati and Otto last week, so I know that they are still here, and still alive—or at least they were a week ago.

One of the men who runs the kitchen fought alongside Vati on the Czech front. I think he and Vati are like Greta and me: they will do anything they can to help each other. He's called Kem. He's in here because he is from the Roma community: one of the few groups of people treated as badly as the Jews.

Kem risked his life to bring a note from Vati. He managed to pass it to Mutti while she was preparing the soup.

Otto and I are fine. Stay strong. Love you always.

We couldn't keep the note, of course. Mutti wanted to. I had to pry it out of her hand.

I went outside and stamped it into the mud, my heart thumping so hard I thought it might beat straight out of my chest. It wouldn't surprise me if that were possible. I have so little flesh covering me that my ribs stick out like a carcass of an animal that has been picked dry by predators.

But now, here, as I fill my mind with everything I can to block out the screams, I thank whatever God I desperately try to persuade myself might exist that I forced Mutti to let me throw Vati's note away.

It could be him in front of us now.

The bile rises with that thought, and I drag my list of good things back to my mind.

Five: Thereza.

Thereza is our cat. Mine and Greta's. She isn't as friendly as Felix and we don't see her as often, but she is always around somewhere.

We named her after—well, it's not hard to see what she was named after. Theresienstadt: our holiday home, our model village, our place of safety where no one will harm us!

Did we ever believe those lies? The lies they fed us before we came here and the lies they still spin to the world out there. There are tiny parts of this place that look almost like a holiday camp. Whenever anyone comes to inspect, that is where the guards take them. That is what they show the world. *See, this is how we treat the Jews. We're doing nothing wrong. They are happy here.*

Everything about this place is a lie.

After Mutti and Greta, Thereza is the best thing about life here. She sneaks through the barracks, up and down the lanes, jumping over the walls in a way that makes my heart hurt with jealousy.

But mostly with love.

She is so tiny you would think she were a kitten, but I don't think she is. I think she just has no home, no mother, no one to feed her.

And in that respect, she is even worse off than we are.

So I make sure that I save at least something for her every day. I save the scraps under our mattress. It's a dangerous thing to do because it encourages rats. But so far, I've managed to give Thereza some carrot peel, a tiny piece of potato, and one time, a few crumbs of bread.

I could get more if I was like some of the people in here. At mealtimes, sometimes you have to pretend that you can't see the lengths people go to in order to try to get some nutrition into their bodies.

I've seen some of the older women plunge into the empty vats, scraping them with spoons to find one more mouthful. I've even seen women scrape the food table with their knives, searching for one last crumb.

Mutti nudges me and tells me not to look when they do it. "Only by turning away can you give them back the dignity they have forgotten they possess," she says.

I think about it a lot. The idea of turning away. We do it here so the women will not feel their shame exhibited. But what about beyond this place? What about the turning away that is happening out there?

245

Sometimes I feel that the whole world has turned away from us. Not for the sake of our dignity, but to uphold their lives, their rights and privileges. Their lies.

The guards have finished the punishment. The men have stopped screaming. They are both lying on the ground, motionless. One of the guards orders two men to take them away. Then he wipes the sweat from his forehead and addresses us all. "If you received a slip of paper with a number on it last night, you must come to the transport station now."

Mutti grips my hand. I'm grateful for the contact. She grounds me. I squeeze her hand, and then we both let go.

As the crowds fall out in different directions, I already have my good thing for today to share with Greta later: I wasn't one of the ones who received a slip of paper. Another day has passed without being transported.

And it's strange because if you looked around at the life we live here, you would surely think every one of us would want to get away.

And we do. Of course we do. But not on the transport. We've heard stories about the transport. Rumors. Terrible, terrible rumors.

And even with the rats and the lice and the hunger and the punishments and the daily cruelty, we know that as long as we are not on the list for deportation, we can still count ourselves among the lucky ones.

1943

Leo

Mama was sitting on the bottom stair when I woke up and came downstairs.

"Mama, you'll catch a chill. You haven't even got slippers on," I said.

"The postman's late," she said. "He should be here by now. Why isn't he here?"

My heart deflated inside me. Since we heard from Papa last year, she had done this almost every day. Waiting for a letter. Even when she didn't sit on the stairs like this, I could see it on her mind—the anticipation, the tiny flame of hope that we might hear from him again. And every day she was disappointed.

"What if he's dead?" she asked. Long gone are the days when she tried to protect me from the worst of her fears. Long gone are the times when I asked myself which of us needed to be the strong one.

I sat down beside her and put an arm around her shoulders. She felt so small beside me, and not just because I had gotten taller. She was shrinking almost as quickly as I was growing.

"He's not dead," I said.

"How do you know?"

I held a hand against my chest. "I feel it in here. In my heart, I know he's alive."

She leaned her head on my shoulder for a moment, and then—

"The postman's here!" Mama jumped up as a shadow walked past the front window.

Yes, there was an envelope coming through the door. Mama was there ready to grab it before it had even come through the mail slot.

I prepared myself. I knew what was about to happen. The same as every other day.

"It's a bill," Mama said. Her shoulders sank so low her whole body seemed to crumple.

Now. Here was my moment. *Tell her. Just tell her. Take her mind off the postman and the bills and the long days without Papa.*

"I've got a girlfriend!" I blurted out. My face burned with embarrassment, and my arms hung stupidly by my sides.

Since Annie and I had met at the cinema last year, we'd become good friends. In many ways, it had felt like having Elsa back in my life. A girl to tease me and laugh with me and share stories of our lives with each other. It felt like a precious gift. Annie had brought a piece of myself back to me.

Then, earlier this year, things had changed between us. We'd been walking in the park on a Saturday afternoon when she stopped and looked at me. And I don't know if it was the sun that caught her hair, the depth in her brown eyes, or just a sudden attack of bravery on my part—but I kissed her.

When the kiss was over, she said, "About time!" and laughed. Then I took her hand, and for the first time we walked hand in hand through the park. I felt that if she hadn't been there, connecting me to the earth, I might have floated up into the sky with happiness.

I'd held off from telling Mama in case it made her sad to remember what it was like to have someone who made you smile—when she didn't have Papa. But last night I'd told Annie that I loved her, and she'd said the same—and I couldn't hold it back from Mama any longer. Surely she wouldn't be sad to know her son was happy. And she needed good news more than ever right now.

She looked at me in silence for half a minute. And then she broke out into the biggest smile.

"Leo! A girlfriend! Oh, my sweet boy!" She held her arms wide and pulled me toward her. I reached down to hug her back.

Suddenly my mother was alive again. "I will put the kettle on, and then you must tell me all about her," she said. "What is her name, how old is she, how did you meet?" She paused to wag a finger at me. "And why are you only telling me now?"

"How do you know I haven't just met her?" I asked, laughing.

Mama raised an eyebrow. "Because I am your mother," she said. "I knew there was something. I have seen a change in you. I didn't know what it was, but now that I do, it is obvious. You have a girl; you have something to live your days for."

As I followed her into the kitchen, I chewed on a nail. "You don't mind?" I asked nervously.

Mama whirled around and took hold of my arms. "Mind? Do I mind?" she asked. "My dearest boy, I could not be happier. This is what I need. Something to feel joyful about."

We sat together at the table, and I told her all about Annie. She was Jewish, like me. She was fifteen, like I was. She had come to England on the *Kindertransport* almost five years ago and lived with foster parents ever since. She hadn't seen or heard anything from her parents since they waved her off at a railway station in Berlin when she was ten years old.

"Oh, the poor girl!" Mama put her hands to her cheeks. "Right, I tell you this," she said. "She is to come here for tea tonight. I can't promise anything special—you know how it is with rationing—but I can promise it will be made with love."

"Mama, that would be wonderful. Thank you."

Mama's eyes filled with tears, but she was smiling. "Oh, I can't wait to have another woman in the family."

I laughed. "It's only been a few months. We haven't exactly gotten married yet!"

Mama patted my hand. "A few months! I can't believe you kept it from me this long. Well, we will make amends tonight."

I leaned over and hugged her tightly. "Thank you, Mama," I said. "I can't wait for Annie to meet you."

She hugged me back. And I whispered in her ear, "And she will meet Papa one day. I promise you she will."

Max

When Max's father told him that they were moving again, he didn't know what to say. He knew what he *wanted* to say. He wanted to scream and cry and beg his father not to take them away from this wonderful life.

Munich had become Max's world. He was one of the boys at school that everyone wanted to be friends with now. He and his Hitler Youth pals ruled the corridors. Even some of the teachers had begun to fear them.

And now he was to be taken away from all of it and moved to Poland, of all places! His father had been promoted again and was to become one of the senior SS officers at the largest of the regime's work camps: Auschwitz. It was an honor for his father, but for Max it felt more like a punishment, and he had done nothing to deserve it.

Luckily, Max was so highly disciplined by now that he knew

far better than to argue or show his feelings. So he shut away his frustrations and instead responded in the expected way.

"Thank you, Father," he said. And then, for good measure, and to show that he understood why the move was necessary, he thrust his arm forward and clicked his heels together and added, *"Heil Hitler!"*

His father returned his salute. "You are a good soldier now," he said. "I am glad you understand."

Max took the gift of his father's compliment with him and went to his bedroom. "Good soldier" was the best thing his father had called him since the evening of his fourteenth birthday. It was a rare treasure, and he would keep it along with the memory of the way his father had rested a hand on his shoulder that day too.

But once he was alone, the feelings rose inside him.

Max could feel something stinging in his eyes. No! He would not cry like a baby. He was a man, a proud Nazi. He would deal with his feelings another way.

He softly closed his bedroom door so that he couldn't be heard. Then he grabbed his pillow from the head of his bed. He placed it on his bedroom sideboard and rolled up his sleeves. And then he punched it, hard. And again. Over and over, punch, punch, punch, he hurled his feelings of injustice and frustration into the pillow till they were out of him.

And then, panting, exhausted, and rubbing his hands where they ached, Max carefully put his pillow back on the bed.

He felt lighter. And he knew what he had to do.

Standing in front of his mirror, Max straightened his shirt, flattened down his hair, and checked his necktie. Then he went back into the lounge, ready to hide his feelings once more.

His father put down his newspaper and called Max to him. "Are you ready to take the next step?" he asked Max, peering into his eyes as he spoke.

Max didn't know what "the next step" was, but he knew one thing: he was ready for anything his father had to offer him.

"Yes, sir," he replied sharply.

His father rubbed his chin for a moment. Then, as if agreeing to something with himself, he nodded. "Very well," he said. "I have something to ask you that I hope will make you happier about the transition."

Had his father heard him in his room? How did he know Max was unhappy about it? "Father, I'm not unhappy," he began. "Whatever you—"

His father held up a hand. "I'm still speaking."

Max swallowed the rest of his sentence and waited.

"Do you want a job, Son? Are you ready to work for the regime?"

"Work for Hitler?" Max gasped. "Yes! Yes, sir! I want nothing more than to serve Hitler. I want to give myself to him completely. Nothing else matters to me."

Max's father removed his glasses and looked properly at Max. He seemed to be studying his son, looking for the cracks in his words, the lies in his promises, the hesitation in his commitment.

It seemed he didn't find any of those things because he nodded slowly and said, "I have already spoken to the commandant. I have asked if there is a role for you. And this morning I had word. You can't do official work there till you are sixteen, so we shall keep quiet about your age. But I will be a senior officer and you have shown yourself to be a good soldier at Hitler Youth, so they are willing to give you an opportunity to help out."

"At Auschwitz?" Max knew of Auschwitz from conversations at Hitler Youth. He didn't know *exactly* what happened there—it was shrouded in too much secrecy for that—but he knew it was an important place. Perhaps the *most* important place.

"Yes. Nothing major. Desk work, minor jobs. To begin with, anyway. And remember, if anyone asks, you are sixteen."

Max could hardly believe what he was hearing. He was being given the opportunity to work at Auschwitz? He wouldn't be playing soldiers with the boys from school. He would be working alongside real soldiers.

Of course, he would miss his friends in Munich, but he had left friends behind before and survived. And this time, the move would put him at the heart of the world he had built his life around.

"Thank you, Father. That would be fantastic!" Max said.

His father put his glasses on and went back to his newspaper, and Max knew that meant he was dismissed. He went back into his bedroom. This time he didn't want to punch anything. This time the fire in his belly wasn't rage or disappointment. It was the thrill of adrenaline coursing through his whole body.

Suddenly he couldn't wait to get out of Munich. Auschwitz was where he would become a true soldier, body and soul. Auschwitz was where he would put into action everything that he had been building toward for the last five years.

Auschwitz was his destiny.

Elsa

I haven't seen Vati or Otto for weeks. I don't know if they are even still alive. No word from them and nothing from Vati's friend Kem. Mutti says he hasn't been in the kitchen for almost two weeks.

We have no way of knowing what has happened to them, not without risking our lives to find out.

And then the day comes. They no longer bother with the slips of paper at night. The transports are too regular and contain too many people. These last weeks, I feel as though we are living in the center of a revolving doorway. Each day, hundreds come in, hundreds go out, in and out, in and out. And every day, those of us who remain say a small prayer of thanks that we are not being put on the transport.

But today it seems my prayers have run out.

"You're leaving." The words wake me, along with the prod of a rifle in my side. "Pack your bags."

The guard moves to the next bunk. "You're leaving. Pack your bags." And the next, and the one after that.

It seems our whole dormitory is being evacuated.

I gently shake Mutti, who is still asleep. I hate to drag her away from the comfort of her dreams—but it will be worse for her if I don't.

"Mutti," I whisper in her ear. "We have to get up."

She reaches around for my hand. "I heard," she says. Her voice is as lifeless as her body. I worry about her lately. She is so thin that I daren't even put my arm around her at night; I feel as though the weight might break her.

We silently drag our bodies off the bunk, pull on our day clothes that haven't been washed in months, and go through our usual morning routines of checking each other's hair for lice, stretching our aching bodies so that we can move without agony—and then I reach under the bunk for our bags and we start the process of packing our diminishing amount of possessions into them.

A tiny part of me remembers a time when I worried about which pretty dress to pack, how many sparkly pairs of shoes I could fit in a bag. Then it became more about how many practical clothes and mementos I could fit in one case. Now I have nothing pretty, and nothing sparkles. I have a few changes of clothes—all ragged, all filthy. I realize what a fool I was to think that those things mattered. Still, hidden among the clothing is my one treasured possession: the photograph of Leo, Max, and me from what feels like several lifetimes ago.

While I still have this photograph, I can tell myself that the girl in it still exists. She is still in here somewhere.

We are soon gathered in the square, ready to be taken to the transport.

Today's good thing: I don't have the energy to feel afraid. I don't have enough moisture in my body to produce tears.

That's two good things. Greta will be proud of me.

Greta. She was taken—I don't know when. It was weeks ago, but I don't know how many. Time has become impossible to measure.

I stand in the cold, hardly feeling the wind on my cheeks, barely acknowledging the snow on the ground beneath my paper-thin shoes.

I am a ghost of the person I used to be.

But then we are ordered to march and, on the way to the transport, something happens that brings me back to life.

"Elsa! Elsa!"

At first I don't turn. I refuse to give in to the hallucination. The disappointment of it will crush me.

But then Mutti looks at me and I know she hears it too. So I let myself turn in the direction of the voice. And I see him. Like me, he is a pale imitation of the person he once was, but when his eyes catch mine and his face breaks into a smile, I know that it is really him.

Otto. My brother. He is alive.

The joy is so overwhelming I have to clutch my chest. I have barely anything but my ribs there now, and I don't know if they are strong enough to hold the weight of joy in my heart.

As we march, I take Mutti's hand and we move bit by bit through the group. Slowly, gradually, inching toward him. He does the same. It takes him much longer than us because his limp is so pronounced now, but we come gradually closer, and as we do, I realize that it's not just Otto. Beside him, there is a thin, gray, hunched-over man.

This time my heart almost rips in two. "Vati!"

We are together. The four of us. Every fiber of my being aches with a longing to hug them, to hold them close to me and never let them go, but I know I can't. We have seen people kicked and beaten for less. I see in their eyes that they want to do the same. But we know the rules. We know the consequences.

We settle for simply knowing we are all alive and walking together.

Finally we reach the railway track. But there is no train here. Up ahead I can only see cattle cars, a long line of them. I guess we will have to wait for them to move before our train comes.

But the cattle cars aren't moving. In fact—the guards are opening up the carriages and ordering people into them. Shouting and shoving and pushing them in as if they are bags of junk to be packed in as tightly as possible.

The crowd is gradually being pushed toward the cars. Mutti

grabs my hand. I grab Otto's on the other side and see him take hold of Vati's with his other hand.

"Do not let them separate us," Mutti hisses.

And then it is our turn. We are in front of a car that is already so full of people I assume we are to move to the next one. Still gripping Mutti's hand, I turn to look. The butt of a rifle in my side turns me sharply back.

"Get in!" the guard shouts.

How are we meant to get in? The car is full.

We aren't left wondering for long. We are shoved and squeezed and pushed and dragged until we are in. I am slammed against the side, face to the wooden slats. Mutti is beside me. Otto and Vati have gotten separated from us, but if I crane my neck, I can see them. They are in the same car. We are together again, that's the main thing.

I remember the train ride to Theresienstadt and how squashed in we were. But at least that was a train designed for humans to ride in. At least we could breathe.

Still more people are being shoved in. We are packed in so tightly I don't even know if I am standing or merely being held upright by the crush of bodies. And still the guards push more people inside. I crane my neck to see. There is *nowhere* for them to go—can't they see that?

People are being trampled as others squeeze on top of them. People are bent double to fill every single available space. Human beings packed into every tiny inch of a cattle car.

This cannot be happening.

I face the wall and pray for them to stop shoving more people in.

And then, at last, they do. I hear the door slam shut, a bolt slide across, and we are finally full.

There is no space that is not filled with people. Not one bit. I don't know how many hundreds of us are in here, but however many it is, surely there are too many to share the minuscule amount of oxygen in here.

We wait in silence. There is not enough air to speak. Finding a speck of it to breathe is all we can manage to do for now. If we are lucky.

And then a clank, a jolt, a shudder, and we are moving.

The cars move so slowly, grinding along the tracks through a world that has abandoned us. I try to imagine what it looks like out there, beyond this dark, putrid carriage.

I imagine forests and fields. Green grass, red leaves, white snow falling on branches. I fancy I hear the snap of a twig as a squirrel scampers up a tree.

My thoughts are dreams. That world is not real anymore. It doesn't exist. For us, anyway. All that exists for us is this darkness, the sound of people moaning, the last gasps as another person gives up the fight. The stench of sweat from the rest of us, the barely living.

And still we trundle on. I am lucky. There is a tiny gap between the wooden panels in front of my face. If I position my head just right, I can find a pinprick of air. It feels like a gold mine.

On and on and on we go.

After hours and hours, the clanking and the grinding come to a stop. Are we there?

Where is "there," anyway?

The door is opened and guards are outside. "Throw out any dead!" one of them shouts.

He reminds me of the men who used to come down the road with their carts in Vienna, shouting out for scrap metal and odds and ends that people no longer needed.

That is now us.

Bodies are passed between people and out through the door. The Nazis throw them on the ground, and then, as abruptly as they opened, the doors are shut and bolted again.

Even with everything that I have been through, I cannot believe what I have just witnessed.

Someone is talking. Muttering in a low voice.

Others join him, and soon I realize what they are saying.

Yitgadal v'yitkadash sh'mei raba b'alma di-v'ra chirutei.

They are reciting Kaddish. The Jewish prayer of mourning.

I don't know it off by heart, but I've heard it in shul. I listen to the voices as if they are a song, and I close my eyes and imagine that the song can raise us out of this nightmare.

We stop again. Three times. Each time is the same. Bodies removed from the carriage and left on the ground outside.

After the third stop, we have immunized ourselves enough to the horror of it to be grateful for the benefit: we have more room.

265

We can breathe. We can even move a little. Vati and Otto squeeze through to join me and Mutti, and the four of us stand in a huddle together. We don't talk much. There is nothing that we can say to each other to take any of this away.

But we are together. And for now, we know what a precious gift that is.

Max

This is where the new arrivals come in." Max's father pointed at the train tracks. "They are unloaded here and join the selection lines where we sort them according to where they are best suited. Ones on the right will go to the barracks. Ones on the left go over there."

Max looked where his father was indicating. A dusty path led to some buildings. There was smoke coming out of the top of them.

Some instinct stopped Max from asking what happened at those buildings. The same thing that stopped him asking what the stench was. He had to force himself to breathe through his mouth so he wouldn't take too much of it in—but even doing that, he couldn't avoid smelling it. It smelled like rotting carcasses. He had never smelled anything like it.

Swallowing the rising bile in his throat, he followed his father along the platform to the far end, where a group of men were collecting cases.

"Over there is a section that we call Canada." His father waved an arm beyond the end of the platform. "These men are collecting goods to be taken there." There were hundreds of cases on the platform, piled high like small mountains. The men were picking them up, three or four at a time, and carrying them in the direction of the place his father had called Canada.

Max could see the men were all dressed the same. Shapeless, striped uniforms that hung loosely on thin bodies. Most of them had either a yellow star or red triangle on their uniform. Max knew this meant that they were Jews or political prisoners and Communists.

Max's father saw his son looking at the men. "This is efficiency at work," he said.

When Max looked at him blankly, he added, "What happens here is business, Max. Profit, loss. We get our prisoners to help out on our production lines: they get to stay alive, for now, and we get the labor for free. It's a good system, yes?"

"Yes, Father," Max answered without hesitation.

And he wouldn't have given the men much more thought. He had, after all, seen plenty of men like them at Dachau, and seeing them here barely made him flinch. This was the way it was. The way it should be. He understood that.

But then he spotted someone. He knew that face. Even when

the man wasn't looking directly at Max—hadn't even seen him. Even on a body now a quarter of the man he had been, even with the bald head, the hollow cheeks, the lifeless expression, just like all the others who Max had long ceased to see as fellow human beings. He knew that face.

Mr. Grunberg. Leo's father.

Max felt rage stir inside him. Why was this man in front of him again? First Dachau and now here? Had he been sent to taunt him? This ghost of his childhood, following him around wherever he went? How *dare* he?

Then Max pushed his rage down, as a good soldier should, and thought again about the man in front of him. He wasn't a ghost or a joke. No, he was simply a trial. Just like the letters from Leo and that old photograph that his father had made him burn. Max wouldn't have been surprised if his father had brought Mr. Grunberg here himself. Whatever the reason, Max knew what was happening. He was being tested to make sure that he was fully deserving of his place in the regime.

Well, he wasn't going to fail a test like that.

So, before the man caught his eye and forced Max to acknowledge any glimmer of recognition, Max turned away and hurried to keep up with his father.

They walked back up the platform again, and his father pointed at the wooden carriages trundling toward them. "New arrivals," he said. "It's going to get busy here soon. Let's get back to my office and have some lunch."

Max marched beside his father without another word, other than to shout out his "*Heil Hitler!*" salute to each soldier they passed.

And if a tiny voice in his head questioned whether he should have acknowledged Mr. Grunberg in some way, even just with a tiny nod of greeting, a much bigger voice replied: *It was safer this way.* Just as it had been safer to leave Vienna and start again in Munich, all those years ago. Just as it had been safer to burn the photograph and the letters from Leo.

Just as it was safer to lock his memories, his thoughts, and his feelings in a dark place deep down inside him, and throw away the key.

Elsa

We've arrived. After what feels like days inside this cattle car, at last the train stops. The engines have been turned off and our door is opened.

My eyes are assaulted by the daylight, and I cover them with my arm as we are ordered to get out of the car and line up.

Vati and Otto are sent to a line on the other side of the platform, dragged away so rapidly we don't even have time to say goodbye.

Guards are everywhere. "Stand here. You, over there. Move quickly." They pull us by our arms, dragging us into lines.

"Leave your cases here," one of the guards orders, pointing to the edge of the platform. "They will be brought to you later."

We leave our cases where they tell us. A group of men are already coming down the platform to collect them.

A flicker of something comforting arises in my belly. They have people to collect our cases for us? Wherever we are, this place can't be too bad.

The men push through the crowds to collect our bags. As they come toward us, one of them suddenly stops walking—just briefly. He starts again. He's looking straight at me. Why is this man staring at me?

There is something familiar about him. I can't place him. He is bald, his face is like a gray mask with dark hollow cheeks, a striped suit hanging limply off his frame. I have never seen this man before. And yet, I know him. I am sure of it.

He's walking toward me. Before I have time to be scared or try to run away, his mouth is next to my ear. "Elsa, it's me," he says, his voice gruff and urgent. "Leo's father."

I gasp out loud. I can't help myself.

"Shush!" he instructs me sharply. Then he talks quickly. "Listen. This is important. You are seventeen," he says.

"I'm not," I reply. Has he forgotten I am the same age as Leo? He can't have forgotten how old his own son is, can he?

Leo. Is he here? Is the whole family here? Despite everything, a sliver of hope worms its way inside me.

Mr. Grunberg shakes his head. "You are seventeen!" he repeats. "When they ask. You are seventeen."

Before I have time to ask who he means by "they" or why he is telling me to lie, or if Leo is here, he has turned and gone, and taken my sliver of hope with him. The hope was a lie, anyway. I

272

don't want Leo to be here. I don't want any of us to be here.

Mutti is beside me. She hadn't even noticed my conversation or Mr. Grunberg. She is looking over at the men's line. "Where have they taken them?" she asks me in a voice I've never heard before. *Keening.*

"My husband, my son," Mutti says. Her legs give way, and she begins to sink to the ground.

I gently lift her up again. The guards mustn't see her like this. I keep an arm around her waist as we edge forward. "Mutti, we have to be strong," I say, some deep instinct taking over and telling me that I must be in charge now.

"I know," Mutti mumbles, leaning her weight against me. She feels so small. So thin. Fragile. "I just don't know if I have any strength left in me."

I can't reply. My throat is clenched taut. I keep my arm around her waist as we stumble wordlessly along the dusty path.

And then we are near the front of the line. Only a few ahead of us. I don't know what makes me do it, but I quickly turn to Mutti: my darling, beloved mother, my rock, my heart, my world. I take her face in my hands. "I love you, Mutti," I say fiercely.

She looks at me. Her chapped lips form the nearest thing to a smile that they are capable of making. "I love you too," she says, her voice like gravel. "I always—"

"No touching!" The guard screams in my ear so loudly it makes me jump. I reach up to wipe his spittle off the side of my face. He sees me do it, and his face breaks out into a cruel smile. Then he

273

makes a horrible sound in his throat, looks directly into my eyes, and spits again.

I feel it run down my cheek, toward my mouth. His grin is daring me to reach up and wipe it off. I know he will do worse if I do, so I leave it.

Another guard pushes me forward. Mutti is in front of me. Facing her is a tall man in SS uniform. He looks at her for two seconds and then points to the left. "That way."

Mutti glances back at me. I start to smile at her. I want to tell her I love her again. I want to remind her to be strong. I want everything for her in that moment. I want those seconds of her looking at me to last forever.

A guard drags her away and another pushes me forward.

I am standing in front of the tall SS man. His jet-black hair is parted to perfection on one side; his eyes, almost as black, bore into me.

"Age?" he says, appraising me.

I have never lied about anything. Mutti and Vati say it is the worst thing you can do. But I no longer believe that. I have seen so much worse, and I think Mr. Grunberg knows better than Mutti and Vati do about this place, so I clear my throat and say, "Seventeen."

He looks at me for a moment longer, rubbing his chin as he eyes me slowly up and down. I don't like the way he's looking at me. It makes me feel unclean, unclothed. Suddenly he points to the right. "That way," he says, and I am dismissed.

Wait. No. He got it wrong. He sent me the wrong way.

A guard is pulling me away. "Please! My mother," I say, pointing at the line shuffling along a dusty track toward some buildings with a chimney puffing out smoke. I can see her in the middle of the group, her head bowed as she walks, her shoulders hunched over.

As I look, I notice that Vati and Otto have been sent to the same line: Vati a few rows ahead of her, Otto limping heavily beside him. All three of them walking away from me.

Something inside me is breaking.

"You've made a mistake," I say, panic rising like a fire inside my body. "My family is over there. I should be with them."

The guard laughs. "Believe me, you don't want to go that way," he says. And then he gives me a shove with the end of his rifle and indicates for the others walking behind me to speed up. "Come on. Keep moving. You should be grateful. You're the lucky ones!"

I don't feel like a lucky one. I feel like someone who has had everything they have ever known or loved taken away and been told they have to keep on living.

I have nothing. I have no one. I refuse to let him define me as lucky. Today there are no good things.

A woman behind me nudges me forward. "Keep going, before they punish us all," she hisses.

My legs move without asking me if they should. My body lumbers forward. And somehow, my eyes find some moisture from deep inside me. A solitary tear runs down my face. All I can see in my mind is my darling mother being taken away from me, her shoulders hunched, her eyes on the ground.

Mutti!

My heart, my world, my everything.

As I walk, I keep trying not to ask myself where they have taken my family, if I will see them again, what is to become of me. My heart beats to the sound of our steps.

I want Mutti.

I want Mutti.

I want Mutti.

Eventually we get there. Wherever "there" is.

Two guards are standing in front of a black gate. Above the gate, three words: *Arbeit Macht Frei.* Work sets you free.

One of the men unlocks the gate and stands beside it. He thrusts his right arm forward and shouts, *"Heil Hitler!"* to the guard beside me.

"Heil Hitler!" the guard replies.

Then he turns to the rest of us and indicates for us to go inside.

"Home, sweet home," he says as we file past. "Welcome to Auschwitz."

We move, wordless and numb, through the gate.

They call me forward and hold my head as they run a rough razor over my scalp. I watch my hair fall to the ground in clumps of knotted red curls, and I remember Greta telling me that my hair was her favorite thing. I can see her eyes twinkle as she throws back her head and laughs.

Like everyone else, Greta is part of a life that is no longer mine to claim.

I follow wordlessly as we file into the building, where they tell us to undress. We let them push and shove and order us through the showers. We don't react as they dress us in shapeless gowns and burn numbers into our arms.

Afterward, when I no longer have my family, my name, my hair, or my clothes, I realize the final thing has been taken from me: my identity. I am no one.

Something inside me switches off, and I know that the process of dying has begun.

1944

Leo

Annie and Mama were in the kitchen. I could hear them chatting and laughing and gossiping, nonstop. I'd been banished till they told me I could come in.

I'd played along and pretended that I minded. "You see more of my mother than you see of me!" I'd teased Annie when she arrived and hugged Mama before even kissing me hello. But she knew that making Mama happy was the only thing that gave me as much pleasure as making Annie herself happy.

Still. It had been an hour and I was getting bored now.

I knocked on the kitchen door. "Can I come in yet?"

"Two more minutes!" Annie replied.

I stood in the hall and counted the seconds. Finally the door opened and Annie beckoned me in with a smile that she saved only for me.

That smile made my heart flutter and meant that she could banish me for another hour if she wanted to, as long as the waiting would end with another smile like that.

"Come on in," she said, and I followed her inside.

Mama was at the sink, finishing the washing-up. She turned and wiped her hands on her apron. "Ready?" she asked Annie.

Annie replied with a nod, and Mama opened the door of our tiny oven. "I'll let you do the honors," she said, passing the oven gloves to Annie.

Annie put the gloves on and reached into the oven. And then she brought something out on a tray.

At first I thought I must be seeing things.

Maybe it was a mirage, a hallucination. But even if my eyes were deceiving me, my other senses weren't. I knew that smell. I had known it and loved it my whole life.

I stared at them both, my jaw open.

"It's Sachertorte," Annie said.

"I know what it is!" I said. "I just don't know how you did it. The ingredients are impossible to get! Sugar, butter . . . real chocolate?!"

"Remember those shoes you grew out of last month?" Mama asked.

"Yes," I replied, wondering what shoes had to do with anything.

"I swapped them for the chocolate!"

"You what?" I burst out laughing.

"And remember I told you I've been doing some sewing but I didn't tell you what it was for?" Annie asked.

"Ye-e-e-s?"

"Well, it was for this," she confessed. "I was doing it to buy flour and sugar."

"I even managed to get the Stewarts in on it," Mama went on. "They found some almonds in an old tin and gave them to us."

I stared at them both. "But—but I don't understand. Why did you do all that for me? It's not my birthday or anything."

Annie came toward me and slipped an arm around my waist. "Not yours," she said. "Ours. It's our anniversary today. We've been together for a whole year."

I was too choked up to speak. Instead I put my arm around her shoulders and beckoned Mama over. Putting my other arm around her, I kissed first Annie's cheek and then the top of Mama's head.

"I can't believe you've done this," I whispered to them. "Thank you."

We stayed like that for a minute, each of us only too aware of the people in between us who were missing.

"Right, come on, then," Mama said, pulling away before those thoughts crystalized and ruined the moment. "Let's eat it while it's warm."

The three of us sat together at the table, and Mama cut us each a big slice.

I closed my eyes as I ate. I had never eaten anything so wonderful in all my life.

Afterward, as we washed up together, and laughed and played

games around the table, and talked until the room grew dark, I felt like the luckiest man alive.

Bowled over by the beautiful thing they had done for me, I couldn't stop watching the two women in my life.

Mama and Annie.

My heart, my world, my everything.

Elsa

I remember a routine I had, back when I was a child, in a time before Auschwitz, where I had to say one good thing each day.

The memory is like thinking of someone else's life and it hurts like a kick to the stomach. No. I have gotten used to those. It is worse. It hurts like the *final* kick, the one you don't get back up from.

I've seen plenty of those, too. They like us to see it. It's part of our discipline. A reminder.

My mind wanders so much nowadays. It is the only part of me without borders made of electric fences. I envy its freedom.

Can you envy your own mind?

My mind is like those cats Greta and I used to care for. What were their names? I strain my thoughts to remember. These moments are like little tests; I'm pushing myself to check that I am still in there somewhere.

Thereza! Felix! That's it. They would wander in and out at will. At Auschwitz, there is only one way out.

And there is only one good thing.

Greta.

She is my miracle. She is my good thing every day. She is the only thing keeping me alive. She came here even before we did, and yet she has outlasted so many. She will outlast me. There is barely anything of me.

I lie in the night with my thoughts. Four of us packed so tightly on this bunk, and I mustn't move, not even a twitch, or the whole shape becomes impossible. We only move when all of us are ready to move, and the only gift I can give to anyone now is to let them have their dreams for a few more minutes.

We are like feral animals, huddled into each other for warmth. Babies surviving in the wild with no mother.

Mother.

I cannot even think that word without pain. Too late. I see her in my mind's eye, her hunched shoulders as she walks away from me for the last time. Vati and Otto somewhere ahead of her in the same line. My last moment of having a family.

I have to change my thoughts before they break me.

My sleeve. My dress. Touch it. Touch it now.

Being careful not to disturb my bunkmates, I stretch my hand across to the sleeve of my dress. The crinkle of soft card under the material. I run my fingers over it like a blind person reading braille, and my thoughts are calmed.

286

My boys.

He came to me again, just once. Mr. Grunberg. He stole a minute while the guards weren't looking. As he came toward me, he reached out as if to shake my hand.

"Well done on your display yesterday," he said.

Display? What was he talking about? I knew that the SS officers brought girls in to dance for them sometimes. Those who did it always came back to the barracks in tears and never spoke about it. But I had never been called.

I was about to tell him he was mistaken when I realized he had something in his hand.

"Take it," he whispered.

I took his hand, as if to accept the handshake. Between our palms was a piece of card I knew so well—even without looking at it. I knew the creases and the shine and the corner that was frayed.

"I rescued it from Canada," he said.

Canada: the first lie I was told here. The lie handed to an innocent version of myself, a naïve girl who stood on a platform thinking that the nice men were going to bring us our luggage.

We never saw any of it again.

And yet, here was my one precious possession, being given to me by the very person who had taken the photo in the first place!

"Hide it," Mr. Grunberg urged. "Hide it well."

A moment later he was gone.

Greta found me a week later. Two gifts in one week. Our reunion was like—I cannot even say what it was like. It was like finding part of myself again. An essential part. I have known since the moment she found me that I cannot survive a day in here without her.

I don't know what she did, but she managed to get moved to the same barrack. She is one of the three beside me now. We are inseparable. She is my twin.

When I told her about the photograph, she pursed her lips tightly.

"Where is it now?" she asked.

I pointed at the bed. The flea-ridden, moth-eaten scrap of filthy, lumpy mattress we share each night. "Under here."

"Elsa, you have to move it!" she said. "People have been killed for less!"

A day later, she had somehow found a needle and thread. Greta manages things like that. She never tells me how. "I promise, it is safer that you don't know," she had said. "And believe me, you don't want to have to do what I do to get these things."

The haunted look on her face when she said that was enough to stop me questioning further.

That night, we sewed the photograph into my dress. It has stayed there ever since.

Greta is whispering in my ear now. She lies behind me in our nighttime formation. Her arm lies across my body. What there is of it. "Body" feels like too grand a word for the walking skeletons that we have become.

"Elsa, are you awake?" she whispers. "Squeeze my hand for yes."

I reach for her hand and squeeze it.

In an even lower voice, so quiet I have to stop breathing to hear her, she says, "We are escaping. Tonight."

I have to fight every impulse in my body not to leap out of bed and scream, *What?*

Or I would if my body had the energy to leap anywhere. Still. I do not know how to respond, and so I lie there, silent and stiff.

"Did you hear me?" Greta asks.

I squeeze her hand.

"I hadn't told you yet because I didn't want you to be part of the plans. Too dangerous."

I twist my head round as far as I'm able without disturbing the other women in the bunk. "They will kill you," I whisper.

"We will die either way," Greta replies. Then a pause before she adds, "Elsa, we're dead in here anyway. This is not living. Don't answer me now. Think about it, but it's happening tonight and I want you to come."

Only a few minutes later, our day has begun. Bright lights, screaming and shouting from the *kapo*, the woman in charge of our barracks. Dragging ourselves out of bed.

I feel like a woman of ninety years old. Every cell in my body aches: with hunger, cold, muscles too weak to move.

But move we must, and half an hour later, we are out in the yard for the first roll call of the day. My feet are bleeding and covered in scabs as I force them to drag me across the uneven concrete so I can stand in a puddle for hours. Sometimes it is less. Usually more. One time, they kept us out here all day. There were three changes of guard during that roll call. Three times they came to work, did their full shift, and went home.

Home.

Just imagine.

They will find any reason to keep us standing out here longer. If someone hesitates before calling their number: start again. If there is any discrepancy in the numbers: start again. If one person does not call out their number loud enough: start again. If the guards are bored and feel like toying with us: start again.

I have seen people literally die in front of me during these roll calls. When your body has nothing inside it to keep you warm and not enough strength to keep you standing, it is hard to resist the relief that would come from giving up. Giving in. Release.

But today something other than hunger is making me dizzy. A new form of release.

Escape.

Can we do it? I would trust Greta with my life. I know that. We *are* each other's lives. And I know that she is right, I will die here whatever happens. So what do I have to lose?

And just like that, I have decided. I will join them.

My body feels alive with hope and longing. The feeling lasts for—I don't know—maybe minutes? Seconds? I want it to last longer. But this is Auschwitz and we are not allowed hope. The mere suggestion of it is enough for punishment.

And the punishment for this hope, it seems, is instant.

An SS guard has come to join the others in front of us. He whispers something to the two guards already there. One of them bends his head forward to listen. Then he nods sharply. Both soldiers click their heels together and give their *"Heil Hitler!"* salutes.

Then the guard who has just joined the others unfolds a piece of paper and turns to us. "The following numbers, come forward!" he shouts.

A sudden premonition grips my stomach, filling me with terror as women step forward. Even before he calls out Greta's number.

No. *No!*

I watch my friend raise her shoulders, lift her chin, straighten her back. I watch, as if through a mist, as she walks through the crowd to the front. I watch one guard take hold of her while another kicks her in the stomach.

And then I cannot watch any more. I cannot listen. I cannot comprehend. My small act of rebellion is that I refuse to believe what is happening in front of my eyes.

And then it is over.

She is gone. And my last shred of belief—in humanity, redemption, survival, in anything—all of it has gone with her.

Eventually they dismiss us. I cannot walk. I have nowhere to go. I have nothing to hold me in place. The anchor that connects me to the world has gone.

A woman from my barracks takes my arm. "Come, Elsa," she says. Her voice is warm, but I cannot be comforted.

I am the walking dead.

Max

Max started his work shift late in the day. As always, he felt a swell of pride as he marched through the gates and looked up at the words over them: *Arbeit Macht Frei.*

Work certainly had made him free. So much so that he didn't even mind working on his birthday. What better way to serve Hitler than to show commitment like that?

He headed for the quarter that he had started patrolling recently. At first he'd worked in the offices, helping out with whatever was required of him, dealing with paperwork, even making drinks for the officers. Recently his father had managed to get him posted to perimeter duty. He liked the feeling of importance it gave him, and the fact that he had to be alert and ready at all times.

Max listened as Karl, the guard he was taking over from, caught him up on the day's events before handing over to him. There had been some trouble with a couple of the women. They'd been hatching a plan to escape. Luckily, they'd been caught and dealt with.

They wouldn't be any more trouble.

Max and Karl faced each other to give their "*Heil Hitler!*" salutes, and Karl started to move away as Max prepared himself to take up position.

Rolf, another guard Max was friendly with, was calling to him from across the path. "Hey, birthday boy," he said.

How did Rolf know it was his birthday? And did he know that Max was only sixteen today?

Max had done what his father had instructed before they'd come and had never told anyone his real age.

As if Max had asked the question out loud, Rolf said, "Your father tells us it's time for you to handle one of these." With that, he pulled out a pistol from its holster and handed it to Max.

The pistol felt heavy in his hands. As Max studied it, Rolf went on. "You want to see some real action? Not just sitting behind a desk or pacing up and down the perimeter?" he asked.

The tiniest shiver went through him. Rolf and Karl were both in their twenties. They'd been here longer than Max. They talked a lot about things like "real action." Always keen to show how brave they were, how strong, how violent. Max was used to men like

293

them. In many ways he admired them. In many ways, he aspired to be like them.

But sometimes he couldn't stop himself. Sometimes he wondered how much of the talk was real, how many of their words they truly believed—and how many were for the benefit of others.

Sure, he joined in with the talk himself, laughing at jokes he didn't always get, talking louder than came naturally to him, sneering at the prisoners as they lumbered by, heads bowed, ragged clothes hanging off them.

But just occasionally, it was as if the veneer slipped and Max caught a glimpse of something underneath it all. He wasn't an idiot; he wasn't a little boy anymore. They might not tell him directly, but he knew what happened over at the other camp where the chimneys blew out smoke every hour of every day.

He also knew what Karl meant when he said there wouldn't be "any more trouble" with the prisoners who'd tried to escape. What "real action" was likely to mean.

Sometimes, before he managed to check himself, Max allowed a tiny voice in his head to ask questions: Was this what he had yearned for? Was this what being the greater race truly meant?

Then he wondered if he was the only one to think those questions. Or if soldiers like Rolf and Karl sometimes thought the same? Soldiers like his father, even, who had always been committed to Hitler and the *Reich*? Did *he* ever question it all?

He would never know the answers as he knew he could never voice any of his questions. He could never show he had moments of doubt. He could never even hint at it. He was in far too deep for that now.

So he plastered a grin on his face and turned to his colleague. "Absolutely!" he said.

"Attaboy!" Rolf patted Max on the back and returned his smile. The camaraderie melted Max's thoughts, and he felt his body relax. He was one of them again.

Rolf shouted to Karl. "You all right to hang on here for a bit longer before Max takes over?" he asked.

"My wife's cooking my favorite dinner!" Karl complained.

"Ah, come on. We won't be too long. It's a treat for Max's birthday."

"Okay. But I need to be gone in the next fifteen minutes."

Rolf waved a hand. "That'll be plenty of time," he said.

Max and Rolf walked together to Block 11 at the far end of the camp, where another guard, Thomas, was waiting to join them in the courtyard.

Max had never been to Block 11 before, but he knew what happened there.

He forced his legs to march and not betray him by shaking noticeably. He forced his heart rate to slow and his palms to stay dry. And he forced his mind to draw a veil across the thought of what they were about to do.

Instead he reminded himself how lucky he was to be there at all. This was his chance to take another step closer to the heart of the regime; another opportunity to serve Hitler.

And Max knew one thing for sure: there was no greater honor than that.

Elsa

It's late in the day when they come. It isn't even a surprise. I know how it works here. I have known all day that I would be under suspicion. It doesn't matter that I wasn't part of the plan, that I didn't even know of it till this morning.

All that matters is association; retribution; punishment.

A year ago, I wouldn't have believed any of this could be possible. A week ago, I would have fought it. Even a day ago, when I still had Greta, a tiny beating pulse in a hidden corner of my heart would have urged me to resist.

But now? Now I have nothing. I am an empty vessel. They will gain nothing from me, and they cannot take anything from me. There is nothing to take.

So I let them drag me out of the barracks. I walk between them along the wide path in between these hated buildings.

I know this is my death march.

The thought brings relief.

I will never again stand here to call out my number.

I will never hold a dirty bowl in my hands, bracing myself to swallow the thin gruel it contains because it is all I will get to eat that day.

I will never crouch over a dirty puddle, slopping its contents into my mouth because the instinct to avoid the horrors of dehydration pulls at me harder than the fear of disease.

I will never see a beetle scuttle across the ground and curse myself that it can outrun me because otherwise it would have been a meal to outdo all others.

I will never see any of it again. And at this moment, that is my one joyful thought.

"In there." A guard orders me through a gate.

Three guards are waiting inside the courtyard. Two of them have rifles over their shoulders. One is holding a pistol. I look down at the ground.

"Stand over there," one of the guards says, pointing toward a wall at the far end of the courtyard. I have heard about this wall. I know what it is.

And the strange thing is that, as I walk toward the wall, I no longer feel afraid. Greta promised we would escape today, and she was right. I have always known there is only one way to leave Auschwitz.

"Turn around," one of the guards shouts.

I turn to face them.

The guard nudges the one with the pistol. "Here you go," he says with a broad smile. "Birthday present. You get to shoot your first Jew."

The other guard is looking down at his pistol. He seems uncertain, hesitant.

"What are you waiting for?" one of the other guards asks. "It's only a Jew."

His hesitation is making it worse. I want him to get it over and done with. Get this life over and done with.

I look up at him, ready to plead with him to finish me off if pleading will make it happen faster. But then I catch his eye.

And in that moment, everything falls away. The years. The camps, the deaths, the losses. All of it fades to nothing, leaving just one thing behind.

My voice is a dry husk. It takes every scrap of effort I can muster to squeeze the word out of me.

"Max?"

Max

This was it, the moment. The defining moment. Everything came to this. Years of training, hungering to be part of the Nazi regime. To take his place. This was the point it had always been leading to.

So why did he feel so nervous? Why was he standing here questioning whether he could do it?

Was it because it was his first time? Did everyone feel this way the first time? Did they all have to push hard against the instincts that tried to stop them, just that one time? Would it get easier?

Or was there more to it than that? Was the old Max still in there somewhere? He knew that if he did this, it would define him forever. Was that what he wanted?

Underneath his soldier's uniform and his bravado, there was still a boy calling out to be praised, to be loved, to be part of something bigger than himself. Was this *really* how he had wanted it to happen?

Did they all ask themselves these questions the first time? If he just knew that, he could get on with it.

Could he ask the others?

"What are you waiting for?" Rolf asked from somewhere behind him. "It's only a Jew."

No. He couldn't ask. He had to do it.

Rolf was right. *Only a Jew.* He could do this. He braced himself. And then ...

"Max?"

The prisoner spoke.

The word jolted him like a shot of electricity through his body.

It didn't make sense. This bald, filthy, barely standing, twig-thin prisoner knew his name? It wasn't possible.

And yet ...

The voice was familiar. It felt like an itch, way below the surface of Max's skin. A treasure long buried and lost for thousands of years.

"Come on, Max," Rolf urged. He was starting to sound impatient. "We haven't got all day. Karl wants to get home for dinner, remember."

Max wiped his forehead. It was wet with sweat, despite the cold. He took a sharp breath and lifted the pistol. This Jew didn't know him. He was imagining things.

He curled his finger around the trigger. Took aim.

And then she smiled at him.

And even though it was years since he'd seen that smile, even though this prisoner in front of him was unrecognizable from the girl he had played with in Vienna, Max knew her smile like he knew himself. It was like a ray of sunlight breaking through clouds. He wanted to give in to it, sink into it, climb it all the way to the warmth of the sun.

"What are you waiting for?" The guards were shouting now.

Still he held the gun, his finger tight on the trigger, his hand shaking.

Still she held his eyes, pinning him to the spot while the world around them froze.

"Come ON!" The guards were still shouting, somewhere on the other side of all this. Angry now. "DO IT!"

Max's hand shook so much he thought he might drop the gun. *Just squeeze the trigger, just do it.*

But her face was still there in front of him. The face of a girl who had once been the best friend in the world to an innocent young boy called Max. He had once childishly believed he would marry this girl.

Max's chest throbbed with the thought of what might have been; the life he could have led.

Such a different life.

All Max had ever wanted was to fit in. But this? This had never been part of it. Or had it? Underneath everything, had he always known deep down inside that this was where his desire to fit in was going to lead him?

And did it matter either way? The truth was, he had chosen this life as much as it had chosen him, and now he was here, surely there was no turning back.

The gun was slippy against his sweating palm. *Only a Jew.* He could do this.

He tightened his grip on the pistol, crooked his finger against the trigger.

And then she spoke again.

"Max, it's me. Elsa."

Elsa: the name was like a bomb exploding inside him.

Elsa: a firework, coursing through his body, lighting up the parts that had lain dormant and dark for years.

Elsa: his best friend. His first kiss.

And now … and now …

The guards were shouting so loud. Their patience wouldn't last much longer. It didn't matter who Max had once been. This was the Max he was now.

He held the pistol with both hands to try to stop the shaking.

Elsa

oments ago, I didn't believe I had anything to live for. Death meant nothing to me. It was just the end of suffering. And now . . .

His eyes are a bridge into another world. Another lifetime. I can't even think of it as the past because I can barely believe that was my life. But it was a life. And now he is here in front of me and I remember that life is something worth fighting for.

I can't let this happen. I'm not just fighting for myself. It feels bigger than that. Am I fighting for Max? For all of us? If I can remind him who he was—who he must surely still be, somewhere beneath that uniform—then perhaps there is a chance I can believe in something again.

"You don't have to do this, Max," I say quietly enough that the other guards won't hear me.

He has both hands on his pistol. But he is still resisting. How can I find the words to get through to him?

And then I have a thought. I have something better than words.

"Wait! Please! One second!" I beg him.

I need to get it. Need to show him.

He won't shoot me when he sees it. He has to remember. Has to see me.

I don't have long. Fevered and frantic, I pull at my sleeve. My fingers hardly work, they are so weak.

Luckily, my dress is even weaker and the fabric tears easily.

Finally I have it. I pull it away from my ragged clothes. My one remaining possession. The only thing I have left in my life.

I hold it out to him. "Here," I say. "I kept it."

The guards behind him are yelling. Max still has the gun aimed at me. He's holding it in both hands, but his hands are shaking. His forehead is soaked in sweat.

My hand is shaking too as I hold the photograph out to him.

"We thought the world was ours to share," I say. "Remember?"

Max

His eyes had clouded with tears. Still holding the gun, he used his arm to swipe his sleeve across his face. But it was useless as the tears kept coming. It was as though a dam had burst inside him and the tears would flow forever, until they had destroyed everything in their path.

He knew what she was holding.

He thought he had killed his memories when he'd destroyed his own copy. He thought his heart had hardened into a stone, like his father had always wanted.

But here it was again, risen from the flames like a phoenix that was telling him he could fly.

Just like he'd believed he could all those years ago. Up there, standing beside her and Leo on the Ferris wheel.

"You left me," he found himself saying. His voice felt like the gravel under his feet.

He knew that the day Elsa said she was leaving was the day he'd begun to break. The day the dark chasm of his loss had begun to engulf him.

And then he'd lost Leo, and then his home and his city. And then he'd lost himself.

No. That was a lie. He couldn't pretend he had sat back and passively let this happen to him. He had *yearned* to be taken. He'd welcomed it, sought it out. He'd run from the boy he had been, desperate to find who else he could become instead.

All he had ever really wanted was to be loved, to be part of something, to make someone proud.

She took a step toward him. "I'm still here," she said. She was still holding the photo out to him.

"SHOOT HER! NOW!" Thomas was beside him, screaming in his ear.

Was Thomas what Max would become? A monster, a cog in a machine that did nothing but hate and kill, hate and kill, until there was nothing left?

She was holding his eyes. "You don't have to do this, Max," she said.

And she was right. He didn't have to do this. He didn't have to do any of it.

The realization hit him like a bullet. It wasn't work that set you free. It was love. All these years, he'd told himself what he had to do to fit in, to be happy, to earn his place in the world.

Through Elsa's eyes, he finally saw clearly. It was a lie. Every bit of it.

He smiled at her. He almost went to her. So nearly. And then . . .

"Come on, Max," Thomas said. "Don't test me."

Wait. A test. *This was a test.* Just like all the other tests of his true commitment to the regime. This was *the* moment for him to prove himself.

All those questions he had asked himself as he had come to the courtyard. The questions he'd wanted to ask a real soldier. He *was* that soldier. He was the man with the answers.

Of course everyone questioned themselves the first time. Of course they all hesitated. But then they remembered who they were, why they were here.

This was the moment to leave the boy behind forever. This was how he would became a true Nazi.

He lifted his pistol.

Elsa

He knows me. He recognizes me. He won't kill me. I know it in my heart.

The joy is overwhelming. I didn't know that I still had the capacity to feel joy. If someone had told me yesterday that I would ever know this feeling again, I would have called them a cruel liar.

And yet, here it is, filling up my heart.

All those years of surviving, and now it has led us here. Back to each other.

The guards behind him are still yelling at him. Their faces are red, eyes bulging with rage. Max ignores them. He only sees me; I only see him.

He's smiling.

And then the soldier beside him is saying something in his

ear. Max is listening. His smile turns cold, freezes.

The air around me turns cold with it. My skin prickles. I can feel everything change and I know that I've lost him.

He raises his pistol. His hand is shaking.

He takes a step closer, grits his teeth.

And then—

BANG.

Max

Max fell so hard he almost knocked her over.

Her face was a mask of shock and horror as she stared at the guards. "What have you done?" she cried as she fell to her knees beside the boy on the ground.

Rolf had turned to stone. He couldn't speak.

"Rolf!" Thomas hissed. "What *have* you done?"

"I'd had enough of waiting. Someone had to kill the Jew."

"He was about to shoot her!" Thomas said. "And you *didn't* kill the Jew; you killed Max. The son of a senior officer!"

"He—he got in the way," Rolf insisted. "He started walking toward her. I thought he wasn't going to do it."

Thomas looked around them, his face white. "Look. No one is here but us," he said. "Get the pistol."

Max's pistol had fallen away from him when Rolf's bullet had hit him in the head. Rolf grabbed the pistol and took it to Thomas. He already knew what the other soldier was thinking. "He shot himself," he said while Thomas curled Max's fingers around the gun and arranged his arm so that it pointed to his head.

Elsa was still kneeling by Max's side. "You've killed him! You've killed him!" she cried, her tears flowing freely.

The soldiers ignored her and spoke to each other. "He was always weak; everyone knows it. They laugh about it behind Herr Fischer's back," Thomas said. He stood back and examined their work. Yes. That looked real. "They will believe us," he said.

"Stupid fool," Rolf agreed, already believing their own lie. "Killing himself over a filthy Jew."

Finally Elsa turned away from Max. Brushing the dust from her legs, she got up and looked at the guards, her eyes black with rage. She stood tall and straight, her chin lifted up, her tears already drying on her cheeks.

"Do it," she said in a low voice. "I have nothing left. Take the last thing from me. My life. I'm done with it."

And then she closed her eyes. She would not give them that. She would not let them into her soul while they emptied out their own.

It was over.

As she fell, the photograph fluttered to the ground beside her.

Three children who owned the world, smiling at the sky.

Leo

Astrange thing happened today. I was walking with Annie, climbing a hill. We got to the top and stood looking down at the town as the day began to draw to a close.

It felt familiar, and I couldn't work out why. I'd never been up this hill before. I'd never looked down on this town.

And then I remembered. It wasn't this town in my memory. It was Vienna.

I smiled as I thought of that day. My best friends, Elsa and Max. I still thought about them every day. I wished so much that they could have met Annie.

Maybe they *would* meet her one day, when this was all over.

I closed my eyes and I was there with them. That day when we thought the world was ours. We thought we could do anything. Childish dreams. Beautiful dreams.

I felt the warmth of the sun on my face now and didn't want to open my eyes.

And then, out of nowhere, a pain flashed across my chest so fiercely it doubled me over.

"Leo, are you okay?" Annie was crouching in front of me.

I held my hand on my chest and tried to calm my breathing. I nodded. Breathed. Counted to ten.

The pain had moved off. I stood up and took her hand.

"You all right?" she asked.

"Yeah. I'm okay now."

"Look," she said, pointing at two clouds in the sky that had drifted together into one. Light beamed through a tiny break between them, like a hazy white ladder to the sun.

I put my arm around Annie and we stood watching together.

The pain in my chest had gone, but it had left a dull ache behind.

It felt a bit like grief.

Papa

When the orderlies were sent in to do their work, one of them noticed something on the ground beside the girl. He reached down into the mud.

"What are you doing?" one of the others asked him. "You'll get whipped for that."

"I don't care," the man replied.

He wiped the card on his sleeve and stood looking at it. It was a photograph.

The man knew this moment. He knew this photograph. He remembered the laughter of that day. He allowed himself a small luxury. He closed his eyes and let his mind wander.

He thought of three happy children, running and laughing and pointing at a city as if they owned it. And the photographer, the man who lived for other people's smiles, who had plenty of his own to go around—did that man still exist? Beneath these tattered clothes and the body that was little more than a skeleton, was he still in there somewhere?

"Grunberg, come on!" his friend urged him. "We need to get this done and get back before the guards start asking why we took so long."

Mr. Grunberg nodded. But still he kept looking at the photograph. His eyes misted and his throat closed over as he ran his fingers across the face of the boy on the left. His beautiful son. Was he all right? Did he get away? And the boy's mother, his own wife, was she alive?

No. He had to stop. He could not survive such questions.

So he put the photograph in his pocket. And then he stood for a moment saying a quiet prayer, before wiping his eyes and getting back to the job they'd been sent to do.

The gentleness in his hands as he lifted the bodies felt like an act of rebellion in itself.

Leo

It was nearly the end of November and one of those days when you realize that there's nothing much to look forward to for a few months.

The war was over, and after weeks of celebrating in the streets life had pretty much settled down to normality again. A dull normality that always had something missing in our case.

It had rained since I'd woken up: the first day of rain for weeks. And now, midafternoon, it was already starting to get dark. Mama was sitting by the fire, humming softly to herself as she knitted a cardigan. I had just gotten up to take another log out of the basket when there was a knock at the door.

"Who's that going to be?" Mama asked. "Are we expecting Annie?"

I shook my head. "Shall I see who it is?"

Mama had already put her knitting down. "I'll go," she said.

As she got up to go to the door, I picked up one of the logs from the basket. I had just placed it on the fire and was in the process of nudging it into place with the poker when I heard a cry from the hallway.

I dropped the poker and ran into the hall. The door was half open. Mama was in the entryway, crouched over, her hands on her face. She looked like she'd fallen.

"Mama, what's happened? Are you okay?" I rushed to her side.

And then the door opened fully and I couldn't believe what I was seeing.

Standing there, in a suit that was hanging off him, wisps of hair on an otherwise bald head, deep shadows under eyes that were little more than dark sockets, and a thin, sticklike body that I could not equate with the larger-than-life man I knew, was my father.

"Papa?"

I stared at him. I couldn't move. Was he real? Was this really happening?

And then his bruised, chapped lips broke into a smile and he said, "Well, are you going to let me in, Son?" And suddenly the dark, rainy day exploded into sunshine.

"Papa! Papa! It's really you!" I cried, throwing my arms around his neck. "I can't believe it! I can't believe it!"

Papa wrapped his thin arms around me and held me close. "It's true," he said. "I'm really here."

And then Mama was beside us, and we were hugging and

laughing and hugging some more, and he was kissing her all over her face and we were all crying.

Mama took his hand. "Come. Come into the warmth," she said. "Come sit by the fire."

I followed them into the sitting room. We barely spoke. All I wanted to do was drink him in. He was home! He was here. Right here with us. Papa had come home.

But the warm silence quickly started to feel strange. Awkward, stilted. Too heavily filled with questions that we didn't dare ask, experiences we weren't brave enough to share.

The silence grew darker and bigger. It was filling the room.

"Papa, there's someone I want you to meet," I said, as an excuse to get away as much as anything else.

I had to process this new reality, this new father, this broken man who didn't look strong enough to hold all the love I wanted to heap on him.

Mama understood. "Go and get her," she said. "She should be part of this moment."

I gave Papa a quick, awkward hug before leaving them to go and get Annie.

By the time we came back to the apartment, something had changed. My parents were holding hands, looking into each other's eyes in a way I remembered.

Papa stood up as soon as we came in the room and smiled his beautiful Papa-smile at Annie. Mama must have told him about her while I was out.

"So you are the person who has made my son a happy man," he said. He opened his arms out wide, and Annie threw herself into them.

"I can't believe I am meeting you at last, Mr. Grunberg," Annie said.

He held her at arm's length and tutted. "I am not Mr. Grunberg to you," he said sternly. "You are part of my family now. Let's not waste any more time. Please, call me Papa."

And then Annie was crying, and Papa was holding out his other arm for me, and Mama had wrapped an arm around Annie's waist, and the four of us clung to each other: a circle of love in front of the fire.

It was going to be okay. We would get there.

Later, after we'd eaten, Papa leaned toward me. "I've got something for you," he said. He reached into his pocket and handed me a photograph.

No. Not *a* photograph. *The* photograph. It was torn and faded and stained. But the three smiles still shone brightly beneath all that. The smiles that said everything.

I took the photograph from him. I wanted to ask how he'd gotten it, where he found it, why he had it. But his face was closed, and I knew he didn't want me to ask any questions. Not yet.

"Did you see them?" I asked instead. I held my breath while I waited for him to reply. I wanted to know the answer, but I was scared as well.

Papa swallowed hard, then nodded. "I saw them both," he said. He paused for a long time, and then in a voice that sounded as if it were filled with gravel, he added, "They were together at the end."

His words landed on my heart with a dull pain. Not a surprise. Not shock. But the deepest sadness in the world. Sadness for my dearest friends who I would never see again. Sadness for all the children, all the lives, all the families, the losses—it was too much to contain, and I wanted to bend over and keen like a wounded animal.

Mama closed her hand over Papa's. Annie reached out to put a hand on my arm. I stared and stared at the photograph until it blurred from my tears. My dearest friends. One day I knew I would need to ask my papa more, but not now.

"Let's say Kaddish for them," Mama said softly. She got up to bring a candle and matches to the table. "Here, you light it," she said to me.

I struck a match, lit the candle, and put the photograph beside it. And then, together, we said the words of mourning for my friends.

Yitgadal v'yitkadash sh'mei raba
b'alma di-v'ra chirutei,
v'yamlich malchutei b'chayeichon
uvyomeichon uvchayei d'chol beit yisrael,
ba'agala uvizman kariv, v'im'ru: amen.

Later, when Annie had gone home, and my parents had gone to bed, I stayed up. I didn't want to leave the candle alone while it burned. I wanted to stay till the end.

I looked at the photograph, and I was back there. That day, less than ten years ago—but still a lifetime away, a million lifetimes away. The day that a moment of carefree joy made me bump into a stranger. The two seconds that would save my life. The two best friends who had shared my childhood, who had shone a light on everything, who had brought me to life.

The night was closing in.

As I sat and watched, the candle flickered and danced and finally went out.

2021

Leo

A young woman came to see me today. A teacher.

She sat perched on the edge of the sofa in my lounge and looked around the room. I saw her eyes travel the length of the sideboard, taking in my photographs. A lifetime of memories: a wife, children, grandchildren, family. And in the center, the oldest photograph of them all, and the most precious: the three children who thought they owned the world. Two copies of the same photograph, framed together. I never found out what had happened to the third.

I made tea for us, and then I sat in the green armchair in the corner of the room and put a blanket over my legs.

"How can I help you?" I asked her.

She told me there is a rise in fascism in Europe. She said there are refugees dying in their attempts to cross oceans to a place of safety. She asked me to come and speak to her students.

I asked her, why me? What do you want with a ninety-three-year-old man who can barely stand, let alone speak to a room full of people?

She said I was there when it happened.

I told her she was wrong. I wasn't there. I was one of the very lucky few who escaped, who lived, who carried the guilt and the burden of survival through my whole life.

"But you lived at that time," she insisted. "You have much to share with us."

I looked into her young, idealistic eyes. For a moment I saw a flash of Elsa in them. The burning in them lit something inside me.

"I'll tell you what," I said. "I'll make a deal with you."

She smiled. "Go on."

"I'll tell you my story," I said. "But my story is a baton, and in telling it I pass it on to you."

"What do I do with it?" she asked me.

I held her eyes for a long time, to make sure she saw me. Really saw me. "You listen well," I said. "And then you do all you can to make sure it never happens again—to anyone. And where you see injustice, you say so, and you encourage others to do the same. Those are my terms."

She held out her hand to shake mine. "They are fair terms," she said. And then she smiled again. "You've got a deal."

"All right," I said, sitting back. "Here is my story. It starts a long time ago, in a fairground in Vienna in 1936 . . ."

ACKNOWLEDGMENTS

This book has involved help, support, guidance, and feedback from more people than anything I've ever written, and I am hugely grateful to everyone who has been on this journey with me.

First and foremost, a huge thank-you to my dad, Harry Kessler, for providing the inspiration for this book—a story I've wanted to tell for many years—and for being so proud of me for finally doing it. I am so happy to be able to share it with you.

A big thank-you to my mum, Merle Goldston, for always being my first reader, for loving my work, and for making me feel like a superstar for every book I write.

Thank you also to Caroline Kessler for your sisterly support along the way. I am particularly grateful for your advice when I called you in a distressed state from Munich and you told me to use the feelings I was having to understand my characters even better. As always, your advice was spot on and exactly what I needed to hear.

I am lucky to have many writer friends who know what it's like to go through the emotional roller coaster of writing a novel and support each other along the way. There are three fabulous groups: the Folly Farm crew, the ladies of the Sofa, and people of the Place. You are all incredibly special and amazing, and I'm so grateful to have you all.

Among my writer friends, there have been a couple of stars who have shone particularly brightly for me with this book. Inbali Iserles—you were such an important and integral part of this journey for me, and knowing you were there in the background helped me to get through some of the particularly difficult moments. And, Anna Wilson, thank you for your friendship and support. You get me and you get my books without me ever needing to explain anything to you, and I'm very grateful to have you in my life.

Claire Pipkin—thank you for sitting on the sofa in our living room and listening to me tell you the whole story. I think that was the first time I said it all out loud, and you filled me with a belief that it might just work.

Hira Pascoe—thank you for always saying exactly what I need to hear. In particular, thank you for being at the end of a phone when I called you from Prague, crying in the street, and asking you how I would ever get Auschwitz out from under my skin.

A special thank-you to my niece Frankie Stubbs. Frankie, you were such a big part of this for me. You were the person I wanted to talk to so many times; your insights and your ideas and your emotional support were an absolute gift, and I can't think about the experience of writing this book without seeing you in there with me.

My dearest friends, Kerry and Kristina—I don't know how I would have gotten through the Europe research trip without having you at the end of a phone, a video call, a WhatsApp message. Your spiritual wisdom, your loving friendship, and your unquestioning support helped get me through five countries, four concentration camps, a few thousand miles, and many tears! Thank you so much to our BL's.

One of the highlights of that trip was our time in Vienna, where the story—both in my novel and in real life—began. I am hugely grateful to Gerhard Strass. Your private tour of Vienna just for us was so insightful, your company was delightful, and your Third Man Museum is absolutely incredible.

For spiritual guidance and support, I am very grateful to Rabbi Robyn Ashworth-Steen. The fact that we had never met did not stop you from generously giving your time to listen, talk, advise, and support me in this process. Thank you for your generosity and your wisdom.

For expert insights relating to the Holocaust, without which this manuscript would be full of holes, I am enormously indebted to Dr. Jaime Ashworth, Prof. Arieh Iserles, Dganit Iserles, Annie Cohen, and my brother Peter Kessler. I am extremely grateful to have had such expert readers to help me get as many details as possible as accurate and close to reality as I could. Any mistakes still in the text are entirely my responsibility.

I am also very grateful to Anna Lloyd, from the Holocaust Educational Trust, for a series of conversations that helped me become clearer about my responsibilities to young people and helped frame this book in the wider context of Holocaust texts.

There is one person who has been by my side for my entire writing career and who has made me feel lucky and grateful for twenty years. Catherine Clarke: all of your authors, all the publishers who work with you and people throughout the publishing industry know what a special person you are, and I am so lucky to have you in my corner. You have been—as always—an absolute gift throughout this process. Your never-wavering support on every level, your confidence in me and my writing, the way you stand back and let your authors take center stage—you are simply amazing and I will always feel like I hit the jackpot for having you as my agent.

This book was a new adventure for me, and I didn't know who would be publishing it until it was finished. I want to say a huge thank-you to Jane Griffiths, Rachel Denwood, Liesa Abrams, Lowri Ribbons, Laura Hough, Sarah Macmillan, Eve Wersocki Morris, and all the brilliant people at Simon & Schuster for bringing me and my book onto your team with such passion, vision, and commitment. I couldn't have ended up in a more perfect place.

I could not have written this book or gotten myself through a grueling research trip without my wife, Laura, by my side. Laura, you have lived with this book in the background for many years and have provided, as you always do, the most incredible bedrock of support as it came to life. You are my biggest cheerleader, my rock, and the other half of everything. Thank you for every single bit of everything you are and for the team that we are together. Your love makes all of it possible.

There have been many others in the background throughout the process of writing this book, and to anyone not mentioned here by name, please know that I am deeply grateful for everyone and everything that has played a part in this journey. I hope the end product lives up to the support it has had along the way.

A LIST OF RESOURCES AND FURTHER READING

The Holocaust Educational Trust (www.het.org.uk) is the leading Holocaust education organization in the UK. Their website contains details of their programs and projects, as well as a wealth of downloadable resources and lesson plans.

The Wiener Holocaust Library (www.wienerlibrary.co.uk) is the oldest Holocaust memorial institution in the UK. It has a reading room in Russell Square in London that is open to the public. It runs a program of talks, lectures, workshops, and exhibitions and also has a resource for schools, the Holocaust Explained.

The National Holocaust Centre and Museum (sometimes referred to as Beth Shalom) (www.holocaust.org.uk) has a permanent exhibition and educational programs.

The Anne Frank Trust UK (www.annefrank.org.uk) has a range of educational programs and traveling exhibitions, focusing on contemporary lessons to be drawn from the life of the teenage diarist.

The Imperial War Museum London and Imperial War Museum North (www.iwm.org.uk) both have extensive permanent and temporary exhibitions relating to the Holocaust.

The Jewish Museum London (www.jewishmuseum.org.uk) has a Holocaust exhibition based around the life of Leon Greenman, a survivor of Auschwitz born in London. It also has an exhibition on the practice and variety of Judaism past and present.

The United States Holocaust Memorial Museum (www.ushmm.org) has a wealth of resources available via its website, including video and audio testimony, photographs, and film footage.

Yad Vashem (www.yadvashem.org) in Jerusalem is the Israeli Holocaust Memorial Authority. It has a wealth of information, downloadable resources, and documents on its website.

The Auschwitz-Birkenau State Museum (www.auschwitz.org) is a major focus of global commemorative events. Its website has information about the history of the camp and memorial.

The International Holocaust Remembrance Alliance (IHRA) (www.holocaustremembrance.com) is an international body that offers strategic guidance in how the Holocaust is taught and remembered.

The About Holocaust website produced by UNESCO and the World Jewish Congress (www.aboutholocaust.org) has thorough and accessible answers to "Frequently Asked Questions" about the Holocaust.

ABOUT THE AUTHOR

LIZ KESSLER has written more than twenty books for children and young people, including the internationally bestselling Emily Windsnap series. She has an MA in Novel Writing and has been a full-time author for the last twenty years. *When the World Was Ours* has been brewing in her heart for at least half that time. Liz lives in the northwest of the UK with her wife, Laura, and their dog, Lowen.